written, illustrated and designed by

edited by

some fonts provided by nate piekos & blambot

carlos gabriel ruiz

bryan a. hollerbach

pretentious record store guy
created by carlos gabriel ruiz

PRETENTIOUS RECORD STORE GUY MONDO LP
ISBN - 978-0-9894416-1-2
PRETENTIOUS RECORD STORE GUY MONDO LP is published by Brain Cloud Comics, a division of Brain Cloud, LLC.

brain cloud comics

This book is dedicated to Palmer and Joel, two of my favorite pretentious record store guys, who showed me what great music was and instilled me with a life-long love for it.

To Andrew Wood, the Captain Hi-Top, love commander. Hide your mom. Control your sister.

To Amy and Gabriel. Always.

TRACK LIST ▶

pretentious record store guy
mondo lp
SIDE A
IF YOU HAVE TO ASK THEN YOU'RE NOT IN THE KNOW
STEREOPHONIC
EST. 2003

INTRODUCTION

This book shouldn't really exist. It almost didn't. If I had listened to what people said in the beginning, it wouldn't exist.

But here we are, and you're holding in your hands the entire story of *Pretentious Record Store Guy*. It's here, and it's real, and it exists because I never gave up on it. This book might not mean much to you, but it means a lot to me.

Pretentious Record Store Guy was the first ongoing professional comic that I got paid to create; I did a comic strip for my college student newspaper, but that doesn't count, and then I did another in a "real" magazine that was canceled after two issues. Up until that point, all I'd ever received was rejection. I had a ton of comic strips and stories rejected; that's usually how it works (at least that's what people tell me that so I don't feel bad).

Write about what you know, and you can never go wrong. That's about as right as you can be.

So I created *Pretentious Record Store Guy*. I started by setting it at a record store (which I had done in college), about getting older (which I thought I was doing at the ripe young age of 25), and about chasing your hopes and dreams (which I'm still doing). It was also about selling out (or not selling out and staying true to your ideals) and how your notion of what constitutes selling out shifts as you get older and are faced with different responsibilities.

I sent *Pretentious Record Store Guy* out to at least 20 different music magazines. Everyone said, "No thanks" or didn't respond (which is way worse). But a funny thing happened on the way to hanging up the ink pen – for the first time in a long time, someone said, "Yes." It was a great feeling.

It's been a long, strange, roller-coaster ride from the pages of *Playback:STL* in 2005 to the miniseries being published in 2008 - 2011 to the Kickstarter campaign in 2013. I'm happy to have that journey finally completed with the publication of this collection.

It's always hard to look back on the past because all you ever see are the mistakes, the roads not taken, all the things you could (and should) have done better. Then you remember all the good times. When I look back on *Pretentious Record Store Guy*, I'm looking back on large part of my twenties. I see all the mistakes, the things I could have done better, and the different places the story could have gone. I miss the person who wrote this, the person who didn't know what the hell he was doing but thought he had it all figured out. It was a good time.

Is this it? Maybe. It's not a "yes" or a "no." Sometimes, that's all you can hope for.

Stay tuned...

Carlos Gabriel Ruiz
St. Louis, Missouri

1
"BASTARDS OF YOUNG"
OR
"A SHIP WITHOUT A RUDDER IS LIKE
A SHIP WITHOUT A RUDDER"
PRETENTIOUS RECORD STORE GUY

THE KEY TO BEING IN A SCENE IS TO BE SEEN...
YOU DRESS UP IN YOUR UNIFORM AND HOPE ALL THE RIGHT PEOPLE TAKE NOTICE.
YOU WANT TO LOOK COOL BUT NOT LIKE YOU TRIED TO LOOK COOL-- THAT IS THE HARD PART.
NADA SURF
with Rogue Wave
IN THIS TOWN, I AM ALL THE RIGHT PEOPLE. NOT JUST BECAUSE I'M IN A BAND AND NOT JUST BECAUSE I'M SO GOOD LOOKING...
...ALTHOUGH THOSE THINGS HELP.
NO, I'M ALL THE RIGHT PEOPLE BECAUSE I WORK AT A RECORD STORE.
GOSPEL
MUSIC
GOOD MORNING, SUNSHINE!

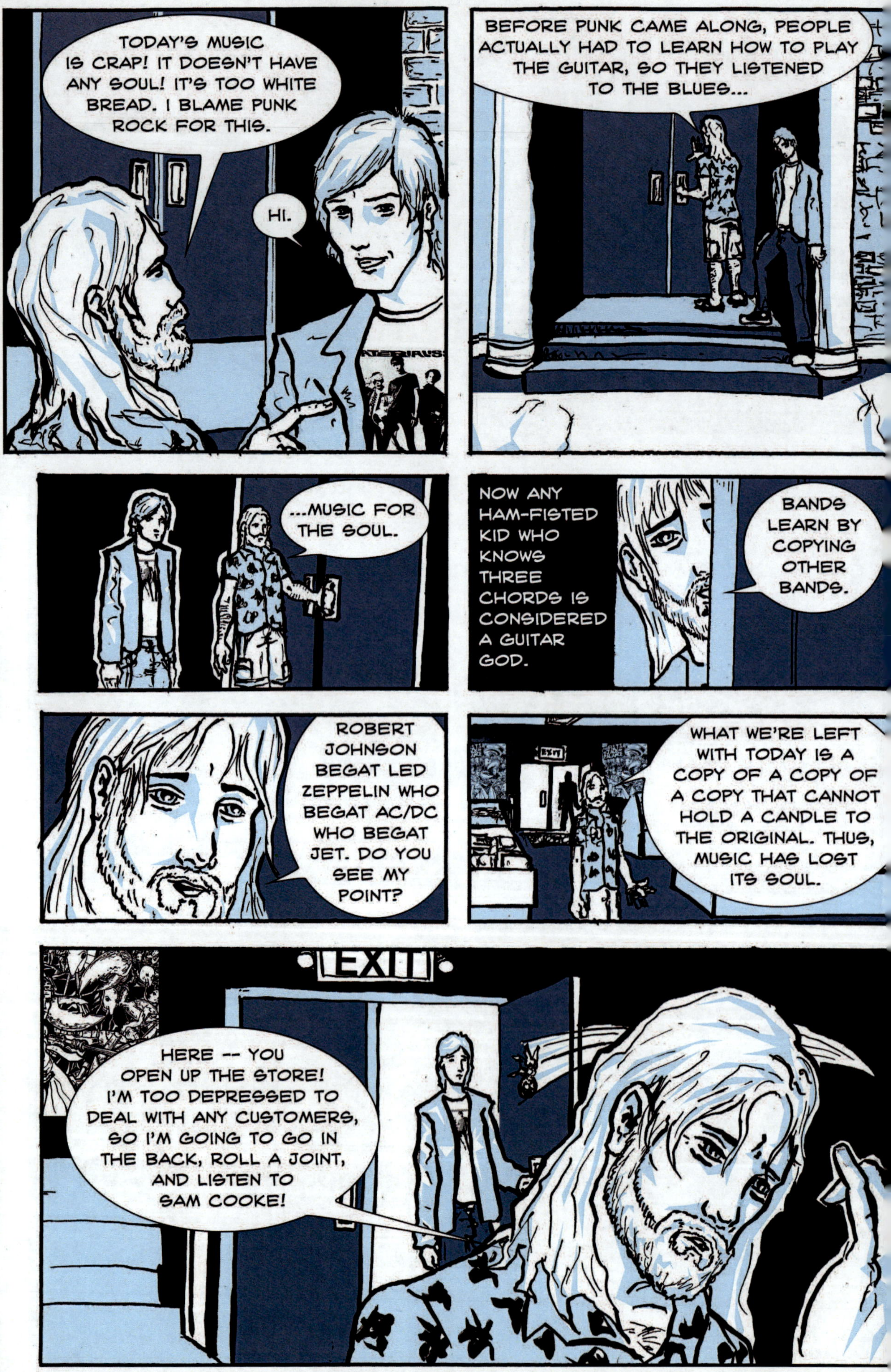
TODAY'S MUSIC IS CRAP! IT DOESN'T HAVE ANY SOUL! IT'S TOO WHITE BREAD. I BLAME PUNK ROCK FOR THIS.
HI.
BEFORE PUNK CAME ALONG, PEOPLE ACTUALLY HAD TO LEARN HOW TO PLAY THE GUITAR, SO THEY LISTENED TO THE BLUES...
...MUSIC FOR THE SOUL.
NOW ANY HAM-FISTED KID WHO KNOWS THREE CHORDS IS CONSIDERED A GUITAR GOD.
BANDS LEARN BY COPYING OTHER BANDS.
ROBERT JOHNSON BEGAT LED ZEPPELIN WHO BEGAT AC/DC WHO BEGAT JET. DO YOU SEE MY POINT?
WHAT WE'RE LEFT WITH TODAY IS A COPY OF A COPY OF A COPY THAT CANNOT HOLD A CANDLE TO THE ORIGINAL. THUS, MUSIC HAS LOST ITS SOUL.
EXIT
HERE -- YOU OPEN UP THE STORE! I'M TOO DEPRESSED TO DEAL WITH ANY CUSTOMERS, SO I'M GOING TO GO IN THE BACK, ROLL A JOINT, AND LISTEN TO SAM COOKE!

EXCUSE ME, BUT DO YOU HAVE THE NEWEST DASHBOARD CONFESSIONAL CD?
I'M SORRY...
INDIE ROCK
NEW RELEASES
BRIGHT EYES
WILCO
Pixies
DID YOU THINK YOU WERE IN A MALL? WE DON'T HAVE ANY OF THAT HOLLISTER, "CRY ME A RIVER BECAUSE MY GIRLFRIEND BROKE UP WITH ME THREE YEARS AGO AND I'M STILL NOT OVER IT" WHINE AND CHEESY, JR. HIGH CRAP! GO TRY THE WAL-MART DOWN THE ROAD!
HOW THE HELL DID YOU KNOW ABOUT MY GIRLFRIEND?
MOJO
!
YOU'RE SEEING HER AREN'T YOU?
MOJO
GET OUT.
GET OUT NOW!
WILCO

GO HOME AND LISTEN TO YOUR MOM'S PHIL COLLINS RECORDS!
PHIL COLLINS IS AMAZING!
BRIGHT EYES
WILCO
Pixies
FUCK PHIL COLLINS!
WHAT THE HECK WAS THAT ABOUT?
THAT KID WAS TRYING TO STEAL A PHIL COLLINS CD, SO I THREW HIM OUT! HE WAS ALSO ASKING ABOUT A BUNCH OF LAME EMO CDs, AND I ASKED HIM IF HE WANTED SOME CHEESE WITH HIS WHINE. KIDS TODAY...
SO WHAT ARE WE LISTENING TO?
THE SMITHS.

KIDS TODAY HAVE NO BAND LOYALTY!
WHENEVER A BAND TRIES TO DO SOMETHING OUTSIDE THE BOX, GROW ARTISTICALLY, OR ATTEMPT TO MAKE A PIECE OF MUSIC THAT IS NOT A BLATANT FACSIMILE OF THEIR LAST RECORD, ALL THEIR FANS ABANDON THEM, AND THE CRITICS CRUCIFY THEM.
THIS COMING FROM A GUY WHO LOST HIS VIRGINITY IN A VW BUG TO SIMON & GARFUNKEL!
SO WHAT?
"SO THAT'S THE SOUND OF SILENCE, HUH?"
ANYWAY... WHEN A BAND WE LIKED WENT ON TOUR WE WENT WITH THEM, SELLING HACKY SACKS, T-SHIRTS, AND GRASS.
EVERYONE CAME TOGETHER LIKE A FAMILY TO MAKE ENDS MEET AND SUPPORT THE BAND.
YOU'RE SUCH A TRUST-FUND HIPPIE. I CAN'T BELIEVE I'M FRIENDS WITH A PHISH PHREAK.
THOSE WERE THE TWO BEST MONTHS OF MY LIFE. THEN I STOPPED SMOKING POT AND REALIZED THAT PHISH SUCKS.
BUT PAUL SIMON WILL ALWAYS BE A GOLDEN GOD.

THERE'S THAT PRETENTIOUS RECORD STORE GUY. MAN, THAT GUY IS SUCH A DICK--
WATCH THIS!
BRIGHT EYES
WILCO
I CAN'T WAIT FOR JENNY'S HALLOWEEN PARTY NEXT WEEK!
DON'T DO IT, MAN! YOU REMEMBER WHAT HAPPENED LAST TIME?
DON'T WORRY, I GOT HIM.
Pixies
HEY, MAN, DO YOU GUYS HAVE ANY OF THE NEWLY REMASTERED AND REPRINTED ACTION LPS ON VINYL? THE ACTION IS THE HEAT.
JUST BECAUSE YOU BOUGHT YOUR FIRST PAIR OF LADIES' JEANS DOESN'T MEAN YOU KNOW ANYTHING ABOUT MUSIC.
CHECK ON ISLE 3.
INDIE
R&B, SOU
THESE AREN'T MY FIRST PAIR OF WOMEN'S JEANS!
YEAH, THEY'RE HIS SECOND.
NEXT TIME YOU WANT TO CHALLENGE ME TO A HIPSTER BATTLE, YOU'D BETTER COME PREPARED.
DICK.
EW RELE

I'M GETTING JADED--
EVEN MORE THAN I USED TO BE.
MAYBE IT'S BECAUSE I'M GETTING OLDER.
GOSPEL MUSIC
I USED TO LOOK FORWARD TO GOING TO A CONCERT AFTER WORK.
THE SESAME ST. WALKERS
with THE WHORE MOANS
M.I.T. MOUSE & MILHOUSE of PAIN
LET'S HAVE A THREE WAY
IT WAS ALWAYS SUCH AN EVENT. I WOULD PLAN MY ENTIRE WEEK AROUND ALL THE DIFFERENT SHOWS.
IT WAS ALWAYS ABOUT THE MUSIC. NOW...
...I'M NOT SURE WHAT IT'S ABOUT ANYMORE.

THE MUSIC BECOMES BACKGROUND.
THE CROWD BECOMES ATMOSPHERE.
REALLY, WHAT'S THE POINT ANYWAY?
SOME BAND, SOME NIGHT, AT LEAST I WAS ON THE GUEST LIST.
BROADWAY
I'M ALWAYS ON THE GUEST LIST.
MAYBE THAT'S THE WHOLE PROBLEM...
...I'M GETTING OLDER, BUT I'M STILL DOING THE SAME THINGS I DID TEN YEARS AGO...

I USED TO DREAM OF PLAYING MUSIC.
MY HEROES WERE ALL ORIGINALS.
IN THE CITY
I HAVE A BAND, BUT WE NEVER PRACTICE ANYMORE UNLESS WE GET TOGETHER TO PLAY ROCK BAND ON THE XBOX. THAT DOESN'T REALLY COUNT, DOES IT?
I'M GETTING TOO OLD TO WASTE WHAT'S LEFT OF MY YOUTH ON HANGOVERS AND SHOWS THAT I DON'T CARE ABOUT. I'M GETTING SICK AND TIRED OF BEING SICK AND TIRED...
SOMETHING HAS GOT TO CHANGE.
I HAVE TO CHANGE.

YOU DRESS UP IN YOUR UNIFORM AND HOPE ALL THE RIGHT PEOPLE TAKE NOTICE.
SOMETIMES YOU JUST NEED A NEW UNIFORM-- A FRESH LOOK.
SOMETIMES YOU JUST NEED A NEW YOU.

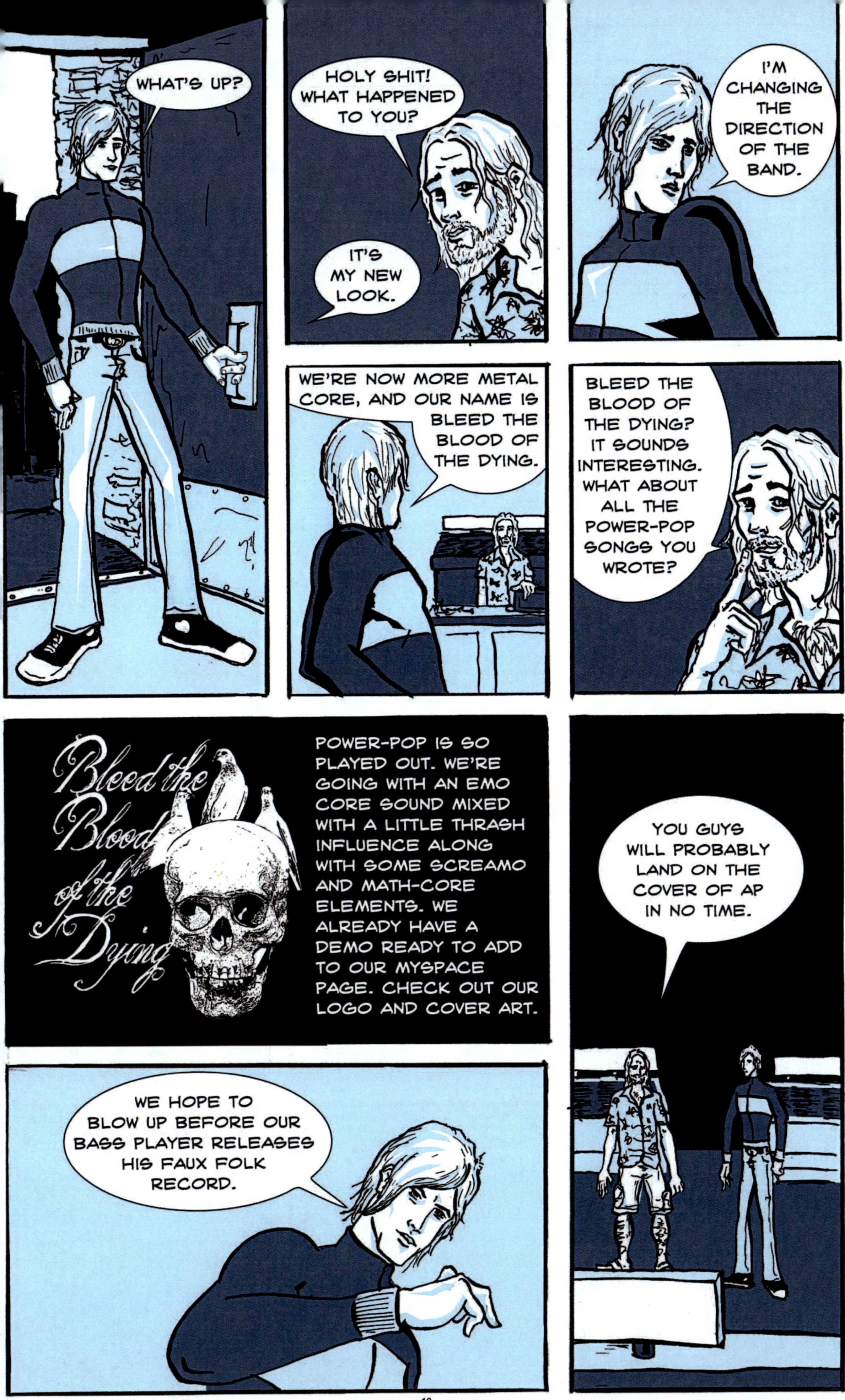
WHAT'S UP?
HOLY SHIT! WHAT HAPPENED TO YOU?
IT'S MY NEW LOOK.
I'M CHANGING THE DIRECTION OF THE BAND.
WE'RE NOW MORE METAL CORE, AND OUR NAME IS BLEED THE BLOOD OF THE DYING.
BLEED THE BLOOD OF THE DYING? IT SOUNDS INTERESTING. WHAT ABOUT ALL THE POWER-POP SONGS YOU WROTE?
Bleed the Blood of the Dying
POWER-POP IS SO PLAYED OUT. WE'RE GOING WITH AN EMO CORE SOUND MIXED WITH A LITTLE THRASH INFLUENCE ALONG WITH SOME SCREAMO AND MATH-CORE ELEMENTS. WE ALREADY HAVE A DEMO READY TO ADD TO OUR MYSPACE PAGE. CHECK OUT OUR LOGO AND COVER ART.
YOU GUYS WILL PROBABLY LAND ON THE COVER OF AP IN NO TIME.
WE HOPE TO BLOW UP BEFORE OUR BASS PLAYER RELEASES HIS FAUX FOLK RECORD.

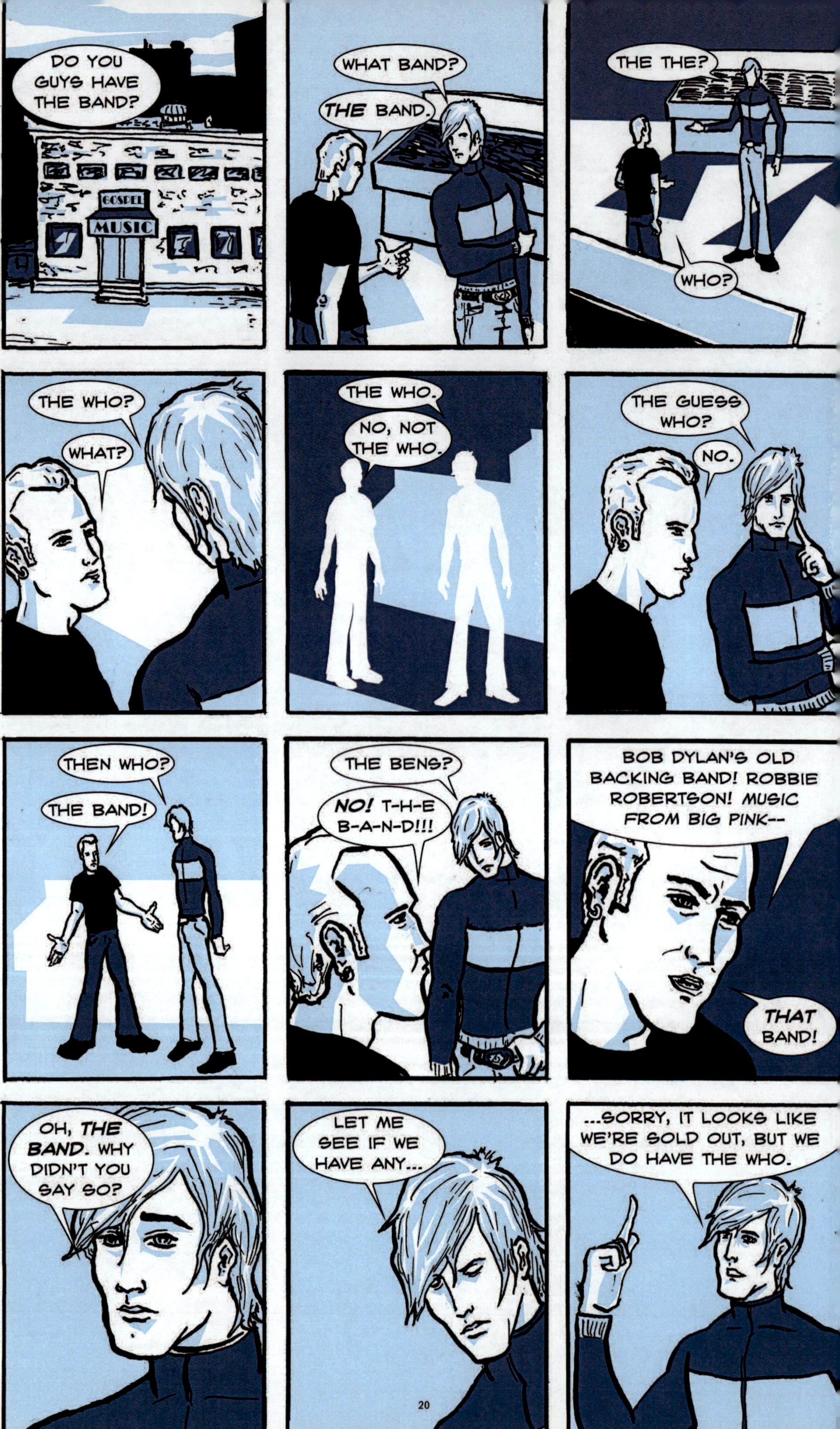
DO YOU GUYS HAVE THE BAND?
GOSPEL MUSIC
WHAT BAND?
THE BAND.
THE THE?
WHO?
THE WHO?
WHAT?
THE WHO.
NO, NOT THE WHO.
THE GUESS WHO?
NO.
THEN WHO?
THE BAND!
THE BENS?
NO! T-H-E B-A-N-D!!!
BOB DYLAN'S OLD BACKING BAND! ROBBIE ROBERTSON! MUSIC FROM BIG PINK--
THAT BAND!
OH, THE BAND. WHY DIDN'T YOU SAY SO?
LET ME SEE IF WE HAVE ANY...
...SORRY, IT LOOKS LIKE WE'RE SOLD OUT, BUT WE DO HAVE THE WHO.

MY NAME IS JONAS
I'M CARRYING THE WHEEL
THANKS FOR ALL YOU'VE SHOWN US
BUT THIS IS HOW WE FEEL

GUESS WHAT I RECEIVED IN THE MAIL TODAY
WHEN I'M PLAYING MUSIC, I'M IN HEAVEN. A GOOD SONG JUST TAKES ME TO THAT PLACE WHERE EVERYTHING IS PERFECT AND MEANT TO BE. I NEVER DID GOOD IN SCHOOL, AND I NEVER COULD THROW A BALL WORTH A DAMN, BUT GIVE ME A GUITAR AND SOMETHING SPECIAL WOULD ALWAYS HAPPEN.
DID YOU HEAR THOSE GUYS IN THERE? THEY SOUND LIKE A REAL BAND! AND THAT SINGER IS SUPER HOT!
THEY *ARE* A REAL BAND, AND I KNOW THE SINGER. I CAN INTRODUCE YOU.
I LIKE THE SOUND OF THAT...

HOW'S IT GOING, PEARL JAM PETE?
OH SAME OLD, SAME OLD, JUST PREACHING THE GOSPEL OF PEARL JAM, WORSHIPPING AT THE TEMPLE OF THE DOG...
...SPREADING THE WORD OF THE GRUNGE MESSIAH, ANDREW WOOD...
...THE LEAD SINGER OF MOTHER LOVE BONE!
FOR HE SO LOVED THE WORLD THAT HE HAD TO DIE FOR THE SINS OF HAIR METAL SO THAT ROCK WOULD BE RESURRECTED BY GRUNGE. SO COME BITE THE APPLE, MY FELLOW STAR DOG CHAMPIONS. HIDE YOUR MOM AND CONTROL YOUR SISTER, AS WE GIVE THANKS AND PRAISE TO CAPTAIN HI-TOP, THE LOVE COMMANDER, ANDREW WOOD! HIS APOSTLES CONTINUE TO SPREAD HIS WORD TODAY, MOST NOTABLY IN PEARL JAM AND TEMPLE OF THE DOG; HIS WILL BE WITH EDDIE. A READING FROM THE BOOK OF STONE.
AMEN, BROTHER!
MAY HE REST IN PEACE KNOWING THAT HIS WORDS STILL RESONATE TODAY.
I'LL DRINK TO THAT.

HEY, WHAT'S UP, GUY? WHAT ARE YOU DOING OUT HERE WHEN ALL YOUR FANS ARE INSIDE ASKING ABOUT YOU?
ME AND PETE WERE JUST HAVING A TALK. HE WAS TELLING ME ABOUT ANDREW WOOD.
THE MESSIAH OF GRUNGE?
WELL, I DON'T WANT TO INTERRUPT YOU TWO, BUT I'VE BEEN MEANING TO TALK TO YOU, GUY--
ARE YOU FIRING ME?
WHAT? NO! WHY WOULD THINK THAT?
BECAUSE I'M ALWAYS RUDE TO ALL OUR CUSTOMERS.
SO?
I JUST WANTED TO TELL YOU THAT I THINK YOU'RE REALLY TALENTED, AND THAT I DON'T WANT YOU WORKING IN THE RECORD STORE YOUR WHOLE LIFE.
YOU'RE STILL YOUNG-- BARELY-- AND I DON'T WANT TO SEE THE WINDOW TO YOUR DREAMS CLOSE UP ON YOU.
DAMN! YOU GUYS ARE BUMMING ME OUT. ENOUGH MALE BONDING FOR ONE NIGHT. WHO'S READY TO DO SOME SERIOUS DRINKING?

THE NEXT DAY...
GOSPEL
Music
GOD, I'M SO HUNG OVER!
THAT'S USUALLY WHAT HAPPENS AFTER TEN TEQUILA SHOTS.
ELEVEN! I WENT TO ELEVEN.
DID YOU EVER THINK ABOUT HOW MAINSTREAM RAP IS ESSENTIALLY TODAY'S HAIR METAL?
HUH? EXPLAIN.
ALL THOSE '80s SONGS WERE ABOUT PARTYING AND DRINKING...
...THEIR VIDEOS WERE FULL OF HALF-NAKED GIRLS DANCING AND SELLING SEX, LIKE ALL RAP VIDEOS. MASCARA AND HAIRSPRAY WERE THE BLING AND BENJAMINS OF THE DAY.
HIP-HOP &
'80s BANDS USED TO WEAR THEIR OWN BAND T-SHIRTS AND SING THEIR BAND'S NAME IN THEIR SONGS. TODAY, RAPPERS WEAR CLOTHES FROM THEIR OWN CLOTHING LABELS, AND THEY NAME-DROP THEMSELVES IN ALL THEIR VERSES. TODAY'S RAP STARS ARE THE NEW BAD BOYS. ALL THE GIRLS ARE ATTRACTED TO THEM JUST LIKE THEY WERE TO THE '80s BANDS. PLUS, TODAY'S RAP STARS ARE ALL COVERED IN TATTOOS AND BUILT-- SO MAINSTREAM RAP IS TODAY'S HAIR METAL.
WELL DONE, SIR.
TOUCHÉ.
THAT'S WHY YOU PAY ME MINIMUM WAGE.

SORRY, KID, BUT WE'RE CLOSED.
BUT THE SIGN SAYS YOU CLOSE AT 10 AND IT'S ONLY 9:45.
LISTEN, KID, I'VE HAD A RAGING HANGOVER ALL DAY LONG. I'M DEHYDRATED AND CRANKY, AND IT'S SATURDAY NIGHT, SO I'M CLOSING! GOT IT?
YEAH, I GOT IT-- YOU'RE AN ASSHOLE! YOU'RE JUST BITTER BECAUSE YOU'RE A 35-YEAR-OLD MAN LIVING IN HIS PARENTS' BASEMENT AND MAKING CRAP AS A CLERK IN A RETAIL STORE. I'D BE UPSET TO, BUT IT DOESN'T CHANGE THE FACT THAT THE STORE SHOULD STILL BE OPEN.
LESS TALKING AND MORE WALKING, OKAY?
DICK.
YOU'RE JUST MAD BECAUSE YOU'RE GOING BALD!

I'M NOT GOING BALD.
AM I?
later...
A FORK IN THE ROAD, WITH THE TWO PATHS AND SO FORTH. IT SEEMS I'VE BEEN STALLED OUT AT THE JUNCTURE FOR A WHILE.
COLLEGE DOESN'T QUITE WORK OUT, SO YOU GET A JOB TO OCCUPY YOUR TIME AND MAKE ENDS MEET.
TIME FLIES. ENDS NEVER MEET. THE MINOR PITSTOP ALONG THE WAY HAS TURNED INTO A MAJOR STAY.
NOW YOUR 20s ARE AN AFTERTHOUGHT, AND YOUR LIFE IS HAPPENING RIGHT BEFORE YOUR VERY EYES. A FORK IN THE ROAD TO NOWHERE GOES WHERE?
WHEN I WAS YOUNG, THE ONLY THING I EVER WANTED WAS TO PLAY MUSIC. I'M NOT SURE WHEN OR WHY I FORGOT THAT ALONG THE WAY.
BOSS

IF EVERYTHING IS NOTHING...
AND NOTHING REALLY MATTERS...
THEN EVERYTHING MATTERS.
HERE GOES EVERYTHING.
HEY, WHAT'S UP, MAN? YOU KNOW, I'VE BEEN THINKING ABOUT WHAT YOU SAID THE OTHER DAY AND--
I QUIT.

2
"LOST IN THE SUPERMARKET"
OR
"ALL THE YOUNG DUDES"
PRETENTIOUS RECORD STORE GUY

somewhere in texas...
1,163 MILES IS A LONG DRIVE.
1,163 MILES IS A LONG, LONG DRIVE INSIDE OF A VAN.
1,163 MILES IS A LONG, LONG, LONG DRIVE INSIDE OF A VAN FILLED WITH PEOPLE YOU BARELY KNOW.
BUT WHEN YOU BARELY EVEN KNOW YOURSELF, HOW CAN YOU TRULY KNOW ANYONE ELSE?
IF THE ROAD TO YOUR LIFE IS LONG, WINDING, AND MOSTLY EMPTY, WHERE DOES IT END UP?
THE ONLY THING I KNOW FOR SURE IS THAT THIS ROAD LEADS ME TO EVERYTHING I'VE EVER WANTED...
WHO CARES ABOUT THE REST?

bleed the blood of the dying
ARE WE THERE YET?
WE HAVE ABOUT 220 MILES LEFT TO GO. NOW PLEASE BE QUIET, AND LET ME FOCUS ON NOT CRASHING. WE HAVE A BIG SHOW TONIGHT.
CAN YOU PLEASE TURN THIS CRAP OFF?
GUY - VOCALS
HUH?
ZACK - GUITAR
DUDE, IT'S PHIL COLLINS' "IN THE AIR TONIGHT"! THIS SONG IS EPIC!
CHARLIE - DRUMS
CAN YOU GUYS KEEP IT DOWN?
REED - KEYBOARD/GUITAR
ZZZZZ!
BARNO - TECH/ROADIE
WHAT'S WRONG WITH PHIL COLLINS?
MATT - BASS
EVERYTHING! PHIL COLLINS STEPPED UP AND MADE A GREAT BAND TERRIBLE AND IN THE PROCESS MADE A FORTUNE BY SWINDLING THE IDIOTIC AND STILL COKED-UP MASSES OF THE '80S.
THEN HE GOES SOLO AND PROCEEDS TO PUT HIS BALDING, BEAT-UP MUG ON THE COVER OF EVERY SINGLE ONE OF HIS ALBUMS.
PLEASE. AS IF THE MUSIC ISN'T ENOUGH TO CAUSE YOU TO IGNITE M-80S RIGHT NEXT TO YOUR EARS TO PURGE THE SOUND FROM YOUR BRAIN, PHIL ALSO WANTS YOU TO VOMIT AS WELL AT THE UNGODLY SITE OF HIS TAUNTING MUG. JERK!

USELESS DRUMMERS NEED TO STAY BEHIND THEIR LITTLE KIT AND LET THE REAL MUSICIANS MAKE THEIR MAGIC. NO OFFENSE, MAN.
WHATEVER.
HERE, PUT THIS MIX TAPE ON INSTEAD OF THAT CRAP. IT'S JAM-PACKED WITH BETTER '80s MUSIC LIKE TALKING HEADS, NEW ORDER, AND THE REPLACEMENTS.
YOUR GENERATION HAS PROBABLY NEVER SEEN A TAPE BEFORE, BUT THEY EXISTED IN THE TIME BEFORE CDS AND MP3s.
IT'S NOT MY FAULT THAT YOU'RE ANCIENT.
I BET YOU ONLY LISTEN TO MUSIC ON VINYL BECAUSE IT REMINDS YOU OF YOUR CHILDHOOD. HOW OLD ARE YOU ANYWAY?
I'M ONLY SEVEN YEARS OLDER THAN YOU BRATS, BUT IT FEELS LIKE A LIFETIME...
I'M STARTING TO SOUND LIKE MY FRIEND...

a few days ago...
SO YOU GUYS ARE REALLY DOING IT, HUH? CONGRATULATIONS ON GETTING BOOKED AT SOUTH BY SOUTHWEST.
YEAH, I STILL CAN'T BELIEVE IT MYSELF. ONE MINUTE WE'RE PLAYING TO CROWDS OF 15, AND THEN THE NEXT MINUTE, SOMEONE HEARS BLEED THE BLOOD OF THE DYING'S DEMO ON MYSPACE, AND WE HAVE A WEST COAST CLUB TOUR AS WELL AS A SPOT AT THE BIGGEST MUSIC SHOWCASE AROUND. WHO'D HAVE THOUGHT?
I KNEW YOU HAD IT IN YOU, GUY. YOU JUST NEEDED TO MAKE THAT LEAP FOR YOURSELF.
SORRY ABOUT LEAVING YOU HIGH AND DRY.
GOSPEL RECORDS WILL BE FINE.
I NEVER THOUGHT THIS DAY WOULD COME. SOUTH BY SOUTHWEST HAS BEEN A DREAM OF MINE FOREVER.
HAVE YOU GUYS WRITTEN MANY SONGS?

SONGS? WE JUST GOT ALL OUR INSTRUMENTS BACK FROM THE PAWN SHOP THE OTHER DAY. WE HAVEN'T HAD A CHANCE TO WRITE ANYTHING ELSE.
WE HAVE FIVE SONGS AND WE KNOW THREE COVERS. THAT SHOULD BE ENOUGH TO GET US THROUGH, RIGHT?
YOU'D BETTER HOPE SO.
LOOKS LIKE YOU'RE ALL SET.
GOOD LUCK, GUY.
REMEMBER TO ALWAYS BE TRUE TO YOURSELF.
THANKS FOR EVERYTHING, MAN. I MEAN IT.
KNOCK 'EM DEAD. I'LL SAY I KNEW YOU WHEN.

austin
ARE WE THERE YET?
WHOA. CHECK OUT THE VIEW--
IT'S AUSTIN, MAN!
WE'RE HERE!
SOUTH BY SOUTHWEST, PREPARE YOURSELF TO BLEED THE BLOOD OF THE DYING.
IS THAT A LINE FOR OUR SHOW? SERIOUSLY?
HOLY SHIT!
I THINK I'M GONNA HURL.

I THINK I SAW ELIJAH WOOD OUT IN THE AUDIENCE.
IT WASN'T ELIJAH WOOD, IT WAS THE KID FROM HARRY POTTER.
I JUST HOPE WINONA RYDER IS OUT THERE.
YOU AND EVERY ASPIRING MUSICIAN IN THE WORLD BECAUSE SHE'S LIKE WILLY WONKA'S GOLDEN TICKET.
ALL RIGHT, GUYS. YOU'RE ON IN FIVE MINUTES. ARE YOU READY?
"ARE YOU READY?" I'VE BEEN WAITING MY WHOLE LIFE FOR THIS. AM I READY? I'VE BEEN READY FOR YEARS...
ALL RIGHT, BOYS, LET'S GO.

AFTER THAT, YOU'RE HOOKED.
THEN YOU'RE JUST CHASING THE DRAGON.
WITH EVERY SONG YOU'
JUST BUILDING ANTICIPAT
FOR THE ROAR OF THE AUDIENCE...

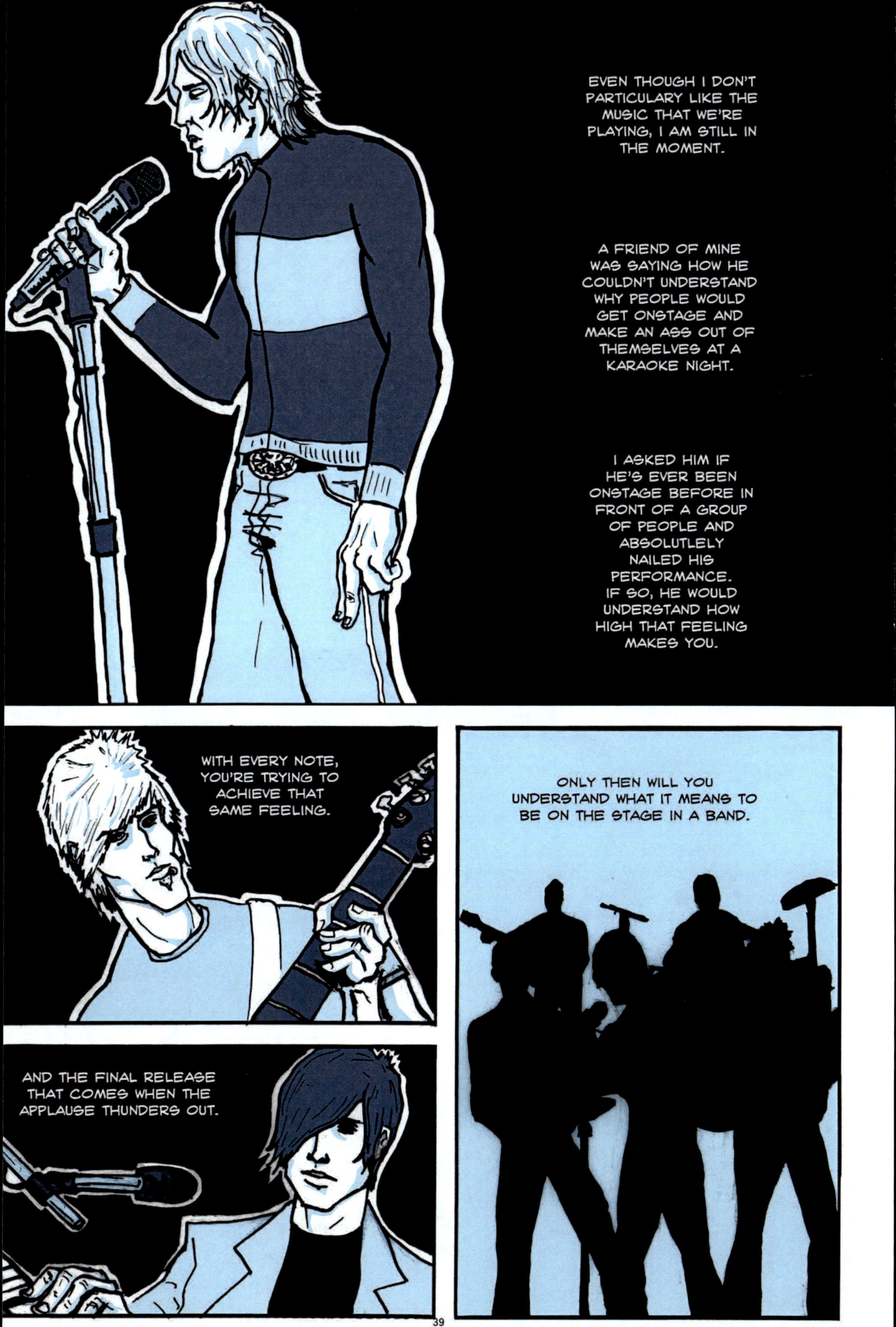
EVEN THOUGH I DON'T PARTICULARY LIKE THE MUSIC THAT WE'RE PLAYING, I AM STILL IN THE MOMENT.
A FRIEND OF MINE WAS SAYING HOW HE COULDN'T UNDERSTAND WHY PEOPLE WOULD GET ONSTAGE AND MAKE AN ASS OUT OF THEMSELVES AT A KARAOKE NIGHT.
I ASKED HIM IF HE'S EVER BEEN ONSTAGE BEFORE IN FRONT OF A GROUP OF PEOPLE AND ABSOLUTLELY NAILED HIS PERFORMANCE. IF SO, HE WOULD UNDERSTAND HOW HIGH THAT FEELING MAKES YOU.
WITH EVERY NOTE, YOU'RE TRYING TO ACHIEVE THAT SAME FEELING.
AND THE FINAL RELEASE THAT COMES WHEN THE APPLAUSE THUNDERS OUT.
ONLY THEN WILL YOU UNDERSTAND WHAT IT MEANS TO BE ON THE STAGE IN A BAND.

DUDE, THAT WAS THE MOST AMAZING SHOW EVER! I'M STILL ON CLOUD NINE WITH HOW AWESOME WE SOUNDED! DO YOU THINK THERE WERE ANY LABEL EXECS OUT IN THE CROWD?
ARE YOU KIDDING ME? HALF THE AUDIENCE WERE WEARING ARMANI SUITS. THAT'S ALL SOUTH BY SOUTHWEST IS ANYMORE, A HIPSTER BATTLE FOR A/R EXECUTIVES
WHAT ARE YOU WRITING?
I'M TAGGING THIS MIRROR.
HIPSTER BATTTLES HAPPEN!
YOU DO KNOW THAT THERE ARE ONLY TWO "T"S IN BATTLE, RIGHT?
OF COURSE. BUT A THREE "T" HIPSTER BATTLE IS MORE EXTREME. YOU KNOW, LIKE TRIPLE X, ONLY IT'S TRIPLE T.
NICE.

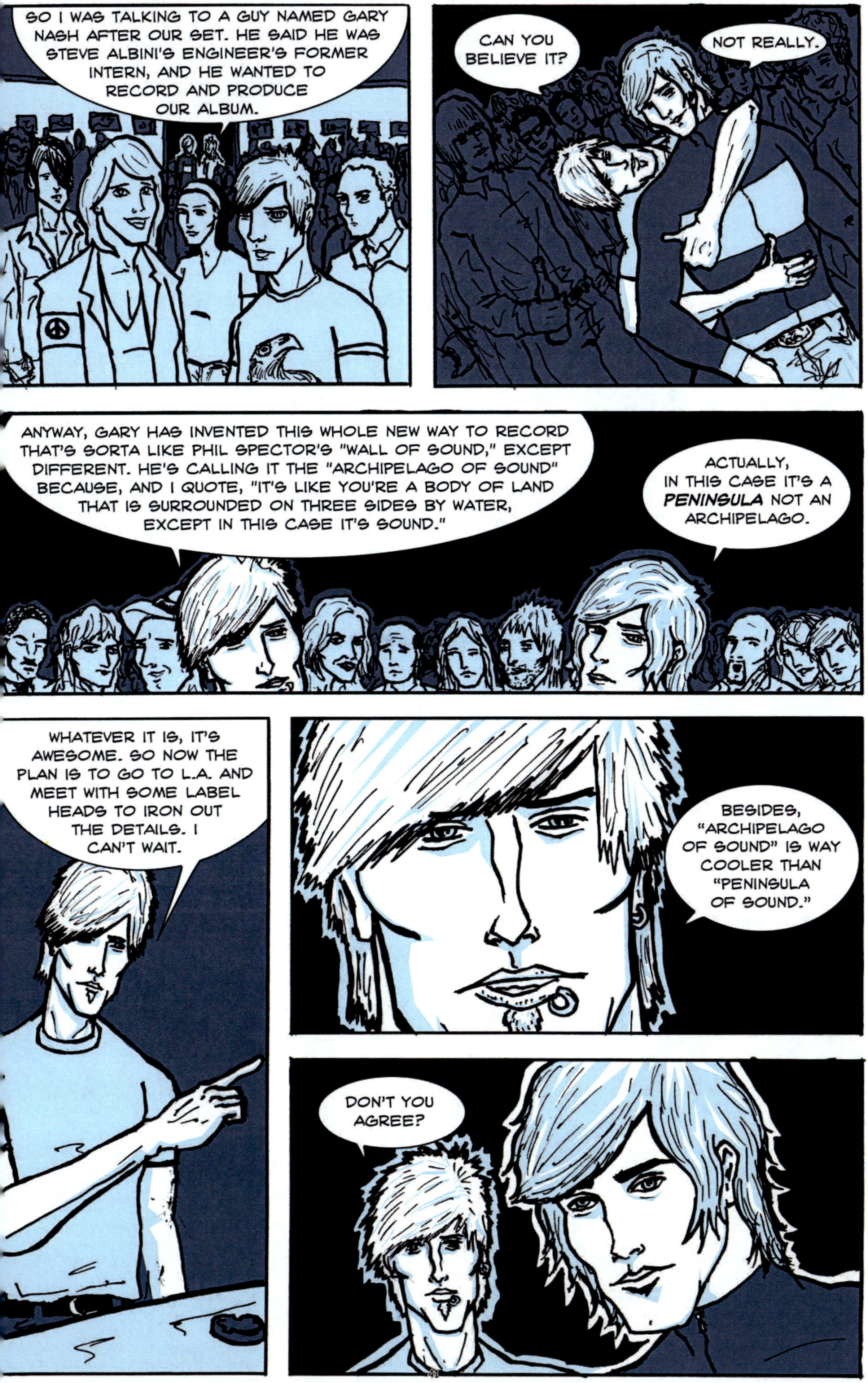
SO I WAS TALKING TO A GUY NAMED GARY NASH AFTER OUR SET. HE SAID HE WAS STEVE ALBINI'S ENGINEER'S FORMER INTERN, AND HE WANTED TO RECORD AND PRODUCE OUR ALBUM.
CAN YOU BELIEVE IT?
NOT REALLY.
ANYWAY, GARY HAS INVENTED THIS WHOLE NEW WAY TO RECORD THAT'S SORTA LIKE PHIL SPECTOR'S "WALL OF SOUND," EXCEPT DIFFERENT. HE'S CALLING IT THE "ARCHIPELAGO OF SOUND" BECAUSE, AND I QUOTE, "IT'S LIKE YOU'RE A BODY OF LAND THAT IS SURROUNDED ON THREE SIDES BY WATER, EXCEPT IN THIS CASE IT'S SOUND."
ACTUALLY, IN THIS CASE IT'S A *PENINSULA* NOT AN ARCHIPELAGO.
WHATEVER IT IS, IT'S AWESOME. SO NOW THE PLAN IS TO GO TO L.A. AND MEET WITH SOME LABEL HEADS TO IRON OUT THE DETAILS. I CAN'T WAIT.
BESIDES, "ARCHIPELAGO OF SOUND" IS WAY COOLER THAN "PENINSULA OF SOUND."
DON'T YOU AGREE?

GUY?
GUY, I'M TALKING TO YOU.
WHO IS THAT?
HI.
HELLO.
DO YOU WANT TO GET A DRINK?

SO WHAT DO YOU WANT TO DRINK?
I DON'T DRINK. I'M NOT STRAIGHT EDGE OR ANYTHING, I JUST LIKE TO BE IN CONTROL OF MYSELF AT ALL TIMES. WHAT ABOUT YOU? DO YOU LIKE TO BE IN CONTROL?
SOMETIMES, BUT SOMETIMES I LIKE TO BE OUT OF CONTROL, TEETERING ON THE EDGE. I LIKE THE FREEDOM THAT IT BRINGS WHEN YOU STEP OUT TO THE LEDGE AND YOU STOP TO LOOK AT THE ABYSS AND CHAOS BELOW.
SO YOU'RE A REBEL WITHOUT A PAUSE, HUH?
I DON'T KNOW WHAT I AM.

IF YOU DON'T KNOW, THEN WHO DOES?
I'M NOT SURE, BUT IT'S HOTTER THAN HELL IN HERE DO YOU WANT TO GET SOME AIR?
ACTUALLY, I *DO* KNOW WHO I AM. I'M GUY VALENTINE AND I'M A SINGER IN A ROCK AND ROLL BAND. GRANTED, MY CURRENT BAND IS A SELLOUT EMO-CORE, THRASH-ROCK KNOCKOFF OUTFIT, BUT I'M STILL THE LEAD SINGER. I SORT OF FEEL LIKE I'M PRETENDING WITH THESE GUYS, AND THAT'S NOT THE TYPE OF PERSON THAT I AM.
REALLY? AND WHAT KIND OF PERSON AM I?
AN AMAZINGLY BEAUTIFUL ONE.

I HAVEN'T HAD THIS MUCH FUN IN A LONG TIME.
YOU'RE STILL BUZZED FROM BEING ONSTAGE IN FRONT OF ALL THOSE PEOPLE.
NO, I'M BUZZED FROM JUST ONE.
WHO COULD THAT BE?

I DON'T WANT TO GET BACK ON THE ROAD TODAY--
SCREW CALIFORNIA AND GARY NASH WITH HIS MISNAMED RECORDING TACTICS. I WANT TO STAY IN TEXAS.
I JUST WANT TO STAY HERE IN BED WITH YOU ALL DAY LONG.
THAT'S SWEET, BUT I DON'T WANT TO BE THE EMO YOKO WHO BREAKS UP THE BAND.
JUST BE SURE TO CALL ME AND TELL ME ALL ABOUT YOUR ADVENTURES...
AUSTIN AND I AREN'T GOING ANYWHERE.
EVER FALLEN IN LOVE WITH SOMEONE?

denver
IT'S FUNNY HOW EVERY CITY IS PRETTY MUCH THE SAME.

seattle
SURE, THEY ALL LOOK A LITTLE BIT DIFFERENT--DIFFERENT BACKGROUND SCENERY, DIFFERENT BUILDINGS--BUT FOR THE MOST PART, THEY ALL HAVE THE SAME ESSENTIAL PARTS.

san francisco
THEY ALL HAVE THEIR GOOD PARTS, THEIR BAD PARTS, AND THEIR UP-AND-COMING PARTS. THEY HAVE THE SAME RESTAURANTS, THE SAME BARS, AND THE SAME TYPE OF PEOPLE IN THOSE BARS.
EXCEPT FOR LOS ANGELES.

los angeles
LOS ANGELES IS LIKE A DIRTY ASSHOLE--THERE'S SHIT EVERYWHERE.

CAPITOL RECORDS
WE ARE ALL SUPER STOKED THAT BLEED THE BLOOD OF THE DYING HAS DECIDED TO SIGN WITH US--
WE KNOW TALENT, AND BOY, DO YOU GUYS HAVE IT IN SPADES!
WHERE DO I SIGN?

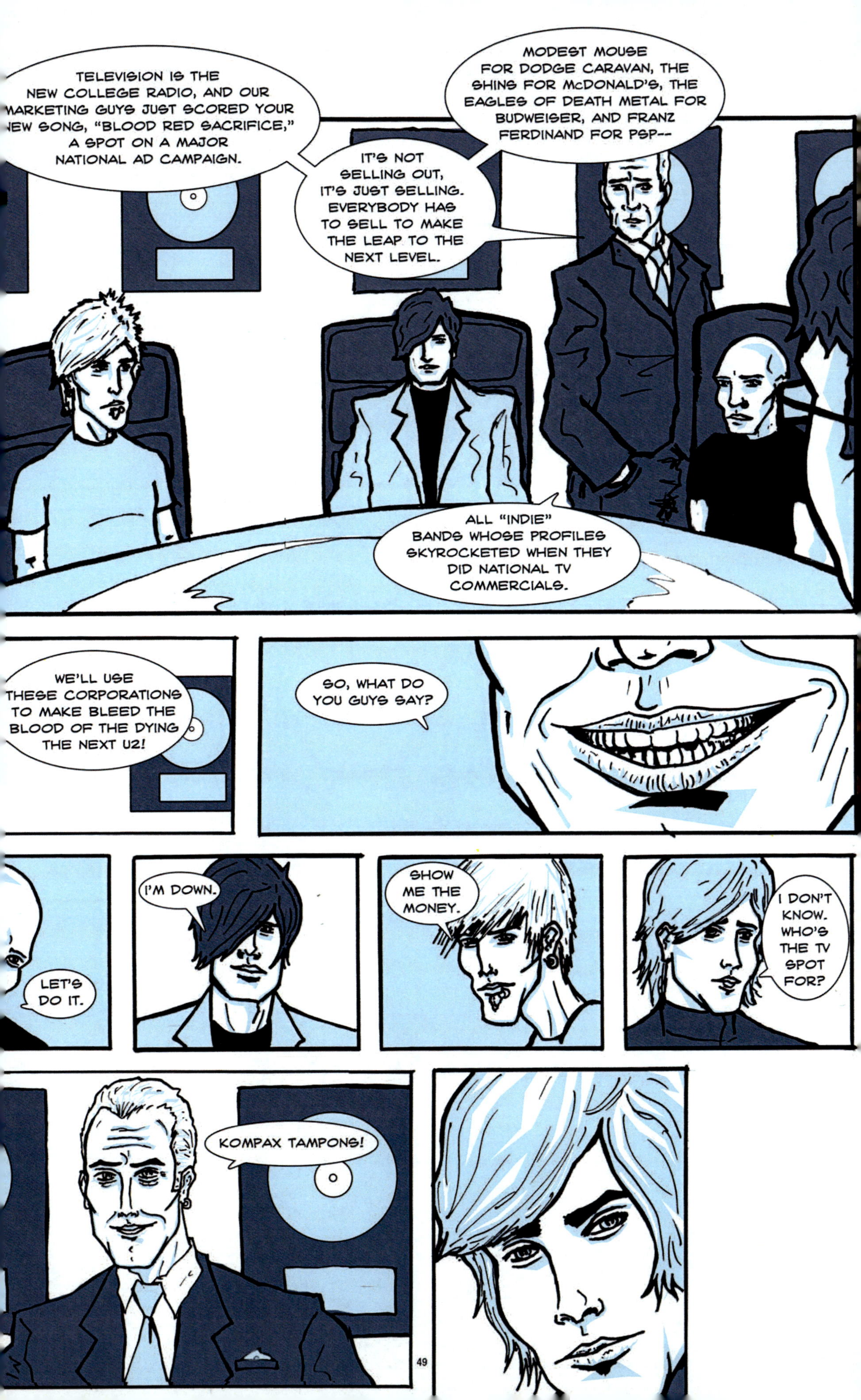
TELEVISION IS THE NEW COLLEGE RADIO, AND OUR MARKETING GUYS JUST SCORED YOUR NEW SONG, "BLOOD RED SACRIFICE," A SPOT ON A MAJOR NATIONAL AD CAMPAIGN.
IT'S NOT SELLING OUT, IT'S JUST SELLING. EVERYBODY HAS TO SELL TO MAKE THE LEAP TO THE NEXT LEVEL.
MODEST MOUSE FOR DODGE CARAVAN, THE SHINS FOR McDONALD'S, THE EAGLES OF DEATH METAL FOR BUDWEISER, AND FRANZ FERDINAND FOR PSP--
ALL "INDIE" BANDS WHOSE PROFILES SKYROCKETED WHEN THEY DID NATIONAL TV COMMERCIALS.
WE'LL USE THESE CORPORATIONS TO MAKE BLEED THE BLOOD OF THE DYING THE NEXT U2!
SO, WHAT DO YOU GUYS SAY?
LET'S DO IT.
I'M DOWN.
SHOW ME THE MONEY.
I DON'T KNOW. WHO'S THE TV SPOT FOR?
KOMPAX TAMPONS!

IS THIS IT?
IS THIS WHAT I'VE WORKED TOWARD ALL MY LIFE?
CAPITOL RECORDS
IS THIS EVERYTHING I'VE ALWAYS WANTED?
MAYBE, BUT DEFINITELY NOT LIKE THIS.
THIS DOESN'T FEEL RIGHT.
THIS ISN'T TRUE.
I WONDER WHAT IT'S LIKE TO BE SECONDS AWAY FROM EVERYTHING THAT YOU HAVE EVER WANTED, ONLY TO TURN AROUND AND WALK AWAY.
I QUIT.
I GUESS I'LL HAVE MY WHOLE LIFE TO FIGURE IT OUT...

3
"IS THIS IT?"
OR
"I WISH IT WAS THE '60s, I WISH I COULD BE HAPPY"
PRETENTIOUS RECORD STORE GUY

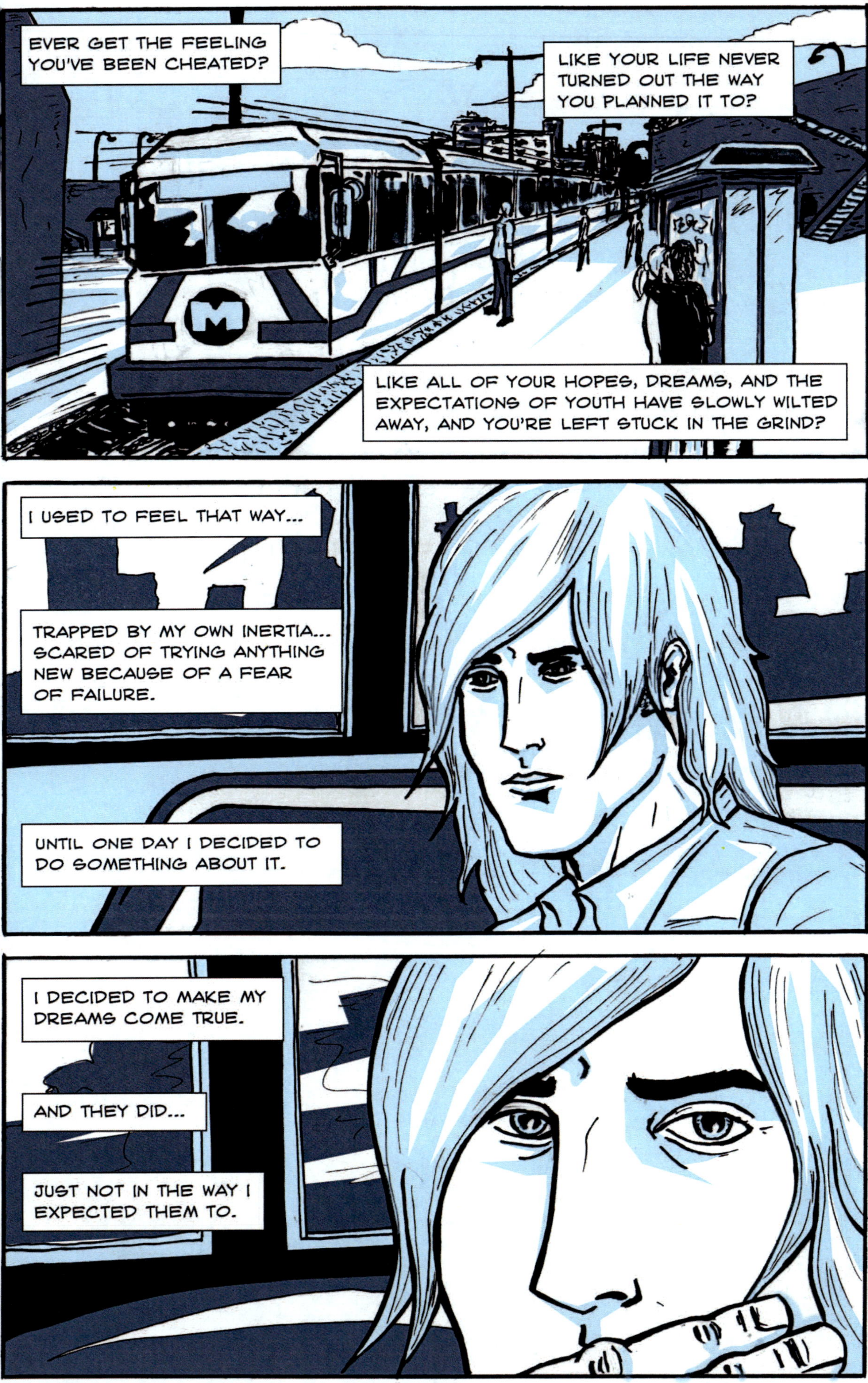
EVER GET THE FEELING YOU'VE BEEN CHEATED?
LIKE YOUR LIFE NEVER TURNED OUT THE WAY YOU PLANNED IT TO?
LIKE ALL OF YOUR HOPES, DREAMS, AND THE EXPECTATIONS OF YOUTH HAVE SLOWLY WILTED AWAY, AND YOU'RE LEFT STUCK IN THE GRIND?
I USED TO FEEL THAT WAY...
TRAPPED BY MY OWN INERTIA... SCARED OF TRYING ANYTHING NEW BECAUSE OF A FEAR OF FAILURE.
UNTIL ONE DAY I DECIDED TO DO SOMETHING ABOUT IT.
I DECIDED TO MAKE MY DREAMS COME TRUE.
AND THEY DID...
JUST NOT IN THE WAY I EXPECTED THEM TO.

SOMETIMES GETTING WHAT YOU WANT ISN'T REALLY WHAT YOU WANTED.
YOU WANTED THE IDEAL, THE NOTION, THE DREAM...
AND IT WAS ALWAYS PERFECT IN YOUR HEAD WHENEVER YOU THOUGHT ABOUT IT.
BUT LIKE MOST THINGS IN LIFE, WHEN YOU PULL THE CAMERA BACK, THE WHOLE PICTURE COMES INTO FOCUS...
AND IT ALWAYS LOOKS DIFFERENT IN THE END.
BECAUSE IN REALITY, NOTHING IS PERFECT.
EVERYTHING IS FLEETING.
YOU JUST HAVE TO KEEP MOVING ON.

THE TRICK IS KNOWING WHEN TO STOP...
...WHEN TO RECHARGE...
...WHEN TO CHANGE THE SCENERY AROUND YOU...
TO HAVE A NEW ADVENTURE...
Strawberry Fields
IN ORDER TO GET A FRESH PERSPECTIVE ON THINGS.
YOU DON'T ALWAYS HAVE TO KNOW WHERE YOU'RE GOING.
Fields
SOMETIMES IT'S MORE FUN TO GET LOST.

THEY SAY YOU CAN NEVER GO HOME AGAIN, BUT THAT DOESN'T HOLD TRUE.
SOMETIMES YOU HAVE TO GO BACK HOME...
IN ORDER TO REMEMBER WHERE YOU'VE BEEN.
THUS RETURNS THE ALL-CONQUERING HERO!
SO HOW WAS L.A.?
TERRIBLE! THE BAND GOT A RECORD DEAL, BUT WE HAD TO SELL OUT IN THE PROCESS. SO I QUIT.
SOUNDS LIKE A TYPICAL DAY IN SUNNY L.A.

YEAH...FUCK L.A.! BUT THE WEATHER WAS REAL NICE.
SO L.A. WAS THAT BAD, HUH?
SORT OF.
IT'S THE CURSE OF BEING ON THE ROAD--IT'LL CHANGE YOU.
I LIKED THE ROAD. IT WAS TOUGH, BUT I LOVED TOURING. PLAYING TO A CROWD OF EIGHT PEOPLE WAS HARD, BUT AFTER SOUTH BY SOUTHWEST, THE CROWDS JUST KEPT GROWING AND GROWING.
THE ONLY THING THAT SUCKED WAS THE MUSIC...
THAT AND GETTING MY HEART BROKEN.

"AFTER I QUIT THE BAND, I DECIDED TO GO BACK TO AUSTIN AND VISIT ZOE.
"I WAS LOVE STRUCK.
"PLUS, I LIKED AUSTIN. IT WAS A COOL TOWN, AND I THOUGHT I COULD DECOMPRESS THERE FOR A WHILE...
"...WHAT COULD POSSIBLY GO WRONG?"
GUY? WHAT ARE YOU DOING HERE? I THOUGHT YOU WERE ON TOUR?
I WAS, BUT I QUIT THE BAND. I WAS THINKING OF YOU A LOT SO I CAME BACK TO SEE YOU.
CAN I COME IN?
UH...NOW'S NOT REALLY A GOOD TIME.
WHO'S AT THE DOOR, BABE?

THIS IS MY FRIEND GUY. HE'S IN THE BAND BLEED THE BLOOD OF THE DYING. AT LEAST HE WAS WHEN THEY WERE IN TOWN A COUPLE MONTHS BACK.
314
"I RECOGNIZED THE SHIRTLESS WONDER IN ZOE'S APARTMENT--HE WAS THE LEAD SINGER FOR THE SESAME STREET WALKERS. I GUESS THEY WERE PASSING THROUGH AUSTIN TOO.
ACTUALLY, I GOTTA RUN. I JUST WANTED TO STOP BY AND SAY "HI." IT WAS GOOD TO SEE YOU.
"I REALIZED THAT I WAS JUST ANOTHER BOY IN A BAND TO HER..."

JESUS! THAT SOUNDS TERRIBLE.
IT WASN'T MY BEST MOMENT.
AND YOU WERE JUST THERE. I WONDER HOW MANY JOCKEYS WERE THERE BEFORE YOU?
THANKS FOR REMINDING ME, PRINCE!
I KEEP TRYING NOT TO THINK ABOUT IT, BUT I APPRECIATE THE FACT THAT YOU LOVE IT SO MUCH.
THE THING IS, I REALLY THOUGHT WE HAD SOMETHING TOO.
SOUNDS LIKE WHAT HAPPENED TO LOU REED.

"THE VELVET UNDERGROUND HAD JUST BROKEN UP, AND LOU WAS LEFT TRYING TO FIGURE OUT WHAT TO DO NEXT...
"NOT ONLY THAT, BUT HE AND NICO HAD BEEN DATING, AND SHE LEFT HIM AFTER GIVING HIM THE CLAP.
"LOU WAS CRUSHED BECAUSE HE'D GIVEN HIS LIFE AND HIS HEART AND SOUL TO HIS BAND, AND HE WAS LEFT PENNILESS, ALONE, AND WITH AN S.T.D.
"HE RETREATED TO HIS PARENTS' HOME ON LONG ISLAND AND BECAME A TYPIST FOR HIS DAD'S ACCOUNTING FIRM...
"SO HERE WAS LOU REED-- THE PROTO-INDIE, HIPSTER VOICE OF HIS GENERATION-- TOILING AWAY IN SOME OFFICE TYPING INSTEAD OF WRITING SONGS AND SINGING.
"UNTIL DAVID BOWIE CAME ALONG AND BROUGHT LOU TO ENGLAND, WHERE BOWIE AND MICK RONSON HUNKERED DOWN WITH REED TO PRODUCE AND RECORD *TRANSFORMER*, LOU'S MOST SUCCESSFUL RECORD, MAKING HIM RELEVANT AGAIN."
YEAH, EXCEPT MY STORY IS A LITTLE DIFFERENT.
WHY? BECAUSE YOU DIDN'T GET AN S.T.D.?
YEAH, THAT'S ONE WAY IT'S DIFFERENT.
BUT I DON'T NEED ZIGGY STARDUST TO SAVE ME.

YOU KNOW, A FUNNY THING HAPPENED ON THE WAY TO NOT SELLING OUT-- I STILL GOT PAID.
I WANTED TO GET OUT OF AUSTIN AS QUICKLY AS I COULD, BUT MY BUS TICKET WASN'T SCHEDULED TO DEPART FOR ANOTHER WEEK.
AFTER PAYING EXTRA TO CHANGE THE DATE ON MY TICKET, I WAS DOWN TO $12 IN MY WALLET AND $32 IN CHECKING.
"I WAS AT THE BUS STOP WAITING FOR THE GREYHOUND...
BUS
"...WHEN MY PHONE RANG."
WHAT'S UP, GUY? I'M HERE WITH THE GUYS, AND WE HAVE YOU ON SPEAKER.
WE KNOW YOU QUIT THE BAND AND EVERYTHING, BUT WANTED TO RUN SOMETHING BY YOU...

SINCE YOU WROTE THE LYRICS AND THE MUSIC TO ALL OF OUR SONGS, YOU'RE THE COPYRIGHT HOLDER....
...WE CAN'T SIGN THE CONTRACT UNLESS YOU ALLOW US TO.
WILL YOU SIGN OFF ON LETTING US USE THE SONGS?
THEY'RE GREAT SONGS, AND WE ALL LOVE THEM. THE BAND'S WORKED REALLY HARD FOR THIS--IT'S EVERYTHING WE'VE DREAMED OF.
ZACH, I--
GUY, IF YOU DON'T WANT TO BE IN THE BAND, THAT'S COOL, BUT PLEASE DON'T RUIN IT FOR THE REST OF US. PLEASE DON'T SACRIFICE--
YOU'RE RIGHT.
YOU GUYS CAN USE THE SONGS--I WON'T STAND IN YOUR WAY.
GO OFF AND BECOME THE ROCK STARS YOU ALWAYS WANTED TO BE.

BY THE TIME I GOT BACK HOME, THE CONTRACT AND THE CHECK FOR THE COMMERCIAL RIGHTS FROM KOMPAX TAMPONS WERE WAITING FOR ME.
I WAITED THREE DAYS BEFORE I SIGNED IT AND SENT IT BACK.
LIKE TOM PETTY SAID, THE WAITING IS THE HARDEST PART.
TO BE IN A SUCCESSFUL BAND IN AMERICA TODAY, YOU ONLY HAVE TO WRITE ONE REALLY GOOD SONG, AND THEN YOU CAN SPEND THE REST OF YOUR CAREER SIMPLY REWRITING THAT SAME SONG.
JUST LOOK AT COLDPLAY OR U2.
DON'T TALK SHIT ABOUT U2, OR I WILL GET VIOLENT.
I LOVE U2, BUT THEY'RE THE BEST WORST BAND IN THE WORLD.
THEY CAN BARELY PLAY THEIR INSTRUMENTS, KNOW ONLY THREE CHORDS, AND ALL OF THEIR SONGS SOUND THE SAME.
SO IF YOU CAN WRITE ONE REALLY GOOD SONG, YOU COULD MAKE A WHOLE CAREER OFF OF IT. I WROTE A BUNCH OF STUPID, IRONIC SONGS THAT GOT ME PAID MORE MONEY THAN I'D EVER THOUGHT I COULD MAKE MY WHOLE LIFE...
WHAT'S GOING TO HAPPEN WHEN I REALLY TRY?

MY OPINION OF U2 ACTUALLY CHANGED WHEN I SAW THEM IN CONCERT.
IN A STADIUM FILLED WITH OVER 70,000 PEOPLE, ALL SINGING THE SAME SONGS THEY HEARD ON THE RADIO, DELIVERED BY THE BEST WORST BAND IN THE WORLD, IT ALL FINALLY MADE SENSE.
IT WAS LIKE GOING TO CHURCH--THE SONGS WERE TIMELESS, THE THEMES WERE UNIVERSAL, AND THE EXPERIENCE WAS SHARED. IT WAS VERY MUCH A RELIGIOUS EXPERIENCE IF YOU BELIEVED IN THE POWER OF ROCK AND ROLL.
I FINALLY GOT U2.
THEN I WONDERED WHAT OTHER PRESUMPTIONS I'D MADE AS A HIPSTER RECORD STORE CLERK THAT I WAS NOW WRONG ABOUT.
I WONDER IF 18-YEAR-OLD ME WOULD THINK THAT I SOLD OUT BECAUSE I SIGNED MY SONGS OVER TO A CORPORATION TO USE IN A TV AD CAMPAIGN.
PROBABLY...
...BUT I DON'T REALLY GIVE A SHIT.

EVENTUALLY WE ALL HAVE TO GROW UP.
AND REAL LIFE IS FULL OF TOUGH CHOICES...
...SELLING THE RIGHTS TO A BUNCH OF SONGS THAT YOU COULDN'T CARE LESS ABOUT ISN'T ONE OF THEM.
THAT WAS AN EASY CHOICE.
AND IT WASN'T ABOUT THE MONEY, ALTHOUGH THAT WAS NICE.
IT WAS ABOUT THE BAND. I WASN'T GOING TO BE THE ONE TO DESTROY THEIR DREAM. WE ALL WORKED HARD TO GET TO THAT POINT, AND IT WOULDN'T HAVE BEEN FAIR OF ME TO STAND IN THEIR WAY.
IT WAS THE BEST DECISION OF MY LIFE.
ONE WAY
EVERYBODY WON AND WE WERE ABLE TO WALK AWAY AS FRIENDS.
HOW MANY TIMES CAN YOU SAY THAT IN LIFE?

THE DYNAMICS OF A BAND ARE A PRETTY INTERESTING THING. USUALLY THERE ARE ONE OR TWO LEADERS, WHETHER THAT BE THE CREATIVE FORCE IN THE GROUP WRITING THE MUSIC AND THE LYRICS OR ITS PUBLIC "FACE."
THE SOCIAL ORDER IS ESTABLISHED EARLY ON, AND RARELY DOES THAT ORDER EVER CHANGE.
STILL, WITHIN THE BAND THERE ARE ALWAYS PEOPLE JOCKEYING FOR MORE POWER.
WHY DO MOST BANDS BREAK UP?
ARGUMENTS OVER MONEY AND THE DISTRIBUTION OF CREDITS...
INTERPERSONAL CONFLICTS AND THE "DIRECTION" OF THE BAND AND MUSIC...
ALL OF WHICH IS USUALLY PLAYED OUT AGAINST A BACKDROP OF DRUG USE/ABUSE AND A VAGABOND LIFE.
IT ALWAYS COMES DOWN TO WHO REALLY HAS THE POWER...
AND WHO WANTS TO HAVE IT.
AS A BAND, YOU'RE ONLY AS STRONG AS YOUR WEAKEST LINK...
...YOU'RE ONLY AS HAPPY AS YOUR LEAST HAPPY MEMBER.
WHO NEEDS THAT AGGRAVATION?

THAT'S WHY I'M GOING SOLO.
THERE'S A CERTAIN AMOUNT OF FREEDOM IN BEING YOUR OWN BOSS.
THE MUSIC CAN BE WHATEVER I WANT IT TO BE--NO ONE'S GOING TO TELL ME WHAT I CAN OR CAN'T DO.
GOOD OR BAD, AT THE END OF THE DAY I'M ON THE HOOK.
I'M GOING ALL IN ON ME.
SO IF I WANT TO SUCCEED ON MY OWN TERMS, I HAVE TO PUT IN ALL THE WORK MYSELF...
...AND NO ONE EVER SAID D.I.Y. WAS EASY.
I WOULDN'T HAVE IT ANY OTHER WAY.

THEY SAY THAT HARD WORK IS ITS OWN REWARD.
THAT'S NOT ENTIRELY TRUE.
THE REWARD FOR HARD WORK IS MORE HARD WORK.
YOU WORK HARD AND YOU BECOME A SUCCESS. CONGRATULATIONS!
NOW YOU HAVE TO GO OUT AND DO IT ALL OVER AGAIN.
YOU ALWAYS HAVE TO KEEP PROVING YOURSELF, EVEN WHEN YOU BECOME SUCCESSFUL--
BECAUSE PEOPLE WILL ALWAYS DOUBT YOUR SUCCESS--UNLESS YOU REPEAT IT.
ONLY AFTER REPEATED SUCCESS WILL PEOPLE FINALLY START TO BELIEVE IN YOU.
UNTIL THEN, YOU HAVE TO PROVE IT.
IT'S A LONG AND WINDING ROAD TO BECOME AN OVERNIGHT SUCCESS.

IMAGINE HOW MUCH WORK GOES INTO BEING A ONE-HIT WONDER.
YEARS OF LEARNING HOW TO PLAY AN INSTRUMENT AND WRITING BAD SONGS, ALL TO GET TO THE POINT WHERE HALFWAY DECENT SONGS START TO EMERGE.
FINALLY EVERYTHING COMES TOGETHER IN THE FORM OF A GREAT SONG.
A LIFETIME OF WORK FOR THREE MINUTES.
MOST PEOPLE JUST HEAR THE END RESULT AND ARE OBLIVIOUS TO WHAT IT TOOK TO GET THERE.
IT'S A WONDER THEY EVEN PERCEIVE THE ONE HIT...
...BUT THEN AGAIN, THAT'S ONE MORE THAN MOST PEOPLE WILL GIVE YOU CREDIT FOR.
DYLAN

YOU ALWAYS REMEMBER THE FIRST TIME...
WHEN YOU HEAR YOUR SONG ON RADIO OR TV.
MINE HAPPENED LATE ONE NIGHT WHILE I WAS CHANNEL-SURFING.
LADIES AND GENTLEMEN! PLEASE GIVE A WARM WELCOME TO YOUR NEW FAVORITE BAND-- BLEED THE BLOOD OF THE DYING!
AND THERE THEY WERE, PLAYING MY SONGS.
IT WAS LIKE AN OUT-OF-BODY EXPERIENCE...
...BECAUSE I REMEMBER THE FIRST TIME WE PLAYED THOSE SONGS ONSTAGE AND HOW IT FELT.
FOR ONE SMALL SECOND, I WONDER IF I MADE THE RIGHT DECISION.

BUT THAT'S JUST JEALOUSY.
IF I AM SUCCESSFUL, I WANT IT TO BE ON MY TERMS.
I DON'T WANT TO BE SOME BULLSHIT TWEEN SENSATION, UNABLE TO WALK THROUGH A CROWD WITHOUT BEING HOUNDED FOR AUTOGRAPHS.
I DON'T WANT PEOPLE FOLLOWING ME AROUND TAKING MY PICTURE EVERYWHERE I GO.
I DON'T WANT FAME.
IT'S ALL SMOKE AND MIRRORS.
WHO KNOW WHAT THE FUCK THE FUTURE WILL BRING?
YOU JUST HAVE TO KEEP MOVING...
AND HOPE FOR SOME INSPIRATION.
"I'VE CHANGED MY HAIRSTYLE SO MANY TIMES NOW, I DON'T KNOW WHAT I LOOK LIKE." -TALKING HEADS
the end.

COVER // ISSUE #1

COVER // ISSUE #2
Bleed the Blood of the Dying
ON TOUR NOW WITH
MERCY BOO COUP
THE SESAME STREET WALKERS
RADIOHEAD
Bleed the Blood of the Dying

COVER // ISSUE #3

A Collection of the Best Pretentious Writings, Blogs and Music Essays from

pretentiousrecord storeguy

Pretentious Record Store Guy's Handy-Dandy Guide to Naming Your Band

Everything you need to know about a band you can find in their name. Naming your band may be the most important thing you'll ever do in your entire life. Give your band a shitty name, and people will automatically think you're shit.

Example: Audioslave – great pedigree, great musicians, shitty band.

How can this be? How can the members of Rage Against the Machine (excellent band, excellent name) and the singer from Soundgarden (equally excellent) end up with sub-par, standard-rock fare? The answer simply lies in the namesake: a rose by any other name would be something else wouldn't it? Call a rose crap, and suddenly something smells like shit. Get my point?

So how can we solve this editorial conundrum?

Glad you asked, because here is **Pretentious Record Store Guy's Handy-Dandy Guide to Naming Your Band**

Rule #1: If you're in any kind of "core" band, you need to show just how tough you really are. Blood works; bleeding works; dying and killing also work. Check out Bleeding Through, A River Runs Red, My Dying Bride, Blood Brothers, etc. So for my post-punk, neo-mathcore, pre-screamo, non-ironic dance band we, named ourselves **Bleed the Blood of the Dying**.

Rule #2: Animals rock. Check out Wolf Eyes, Wolfparade, Wolf Mother, Band of Horses, Horse the Band, The Unicorns, etc.

Rule #3: Puns work. Check out Beatles, Texas Chainsaw Mass Choir, etc. (Well, maybe they aren't puns, but I'm not exactly sure what they are. I graduated high school, but I was mainly incoherent the majority of the time I was there. I've had a few college classes but nothing that has really stuck, you know, so why bother? I already have the best job in the world: record store guy. I get to sit around all day and listen and talk about music, and I get paid for it. How can you beat that? So it might not be a pun, but just because I'm not some English major doesn't mean that you're better than me. Screw you for judging me.)

Rule #4: "The" bands tend to work really well. Simply put "the" in front of something, thus making that something plural and watch the record deals come in (but this tends to only work if your sound is 70's garage rock rounding)... See The Strokes, The White Stripes, The Editors, The Stills, The Hives, etc.

Rule #5: Head(s) always works. See Talking Heads, Radiohead, The Lemonheads, etc.

Rule #6: When in doubt, go pretentious– that is, after all, my main motto in life. Clap Your Hands, Say Yeah, Godspeed You Black Emperor, etc. the longer the title, the cooler it is.

Join the Pretentious Record Store Guy Fan Club

Join the **Pretenious Record Store Guy Fan Club** now (for fans of Indie rock, fashionistas, hipsters, groupies, models/supermodels, models/actresses, and Woody Allen).

Basically the **Pretentious Record Store Guy Fan Club** is a place where fans of *Pretentious Record Store Guy* can go and talk about how great *Pretentious Record Store Guy* is. Say you like a comic or you really, really like a comic, then you can tell people how much you like it. And then I can read how much you guys worship me, and then my ego can expand even more, thus covering up all the insecurity I felt as a totally unpretentious young lad, who because of his frail physique and ridiculous good looks was picked upon by equally insecure philistines and jocks.

If you don't like the comic, then you can just burn in hell; the world really doesn't need your negativity anyway. You probably secretly like *Cathy* and *The Family Circus,* don't you?

Go home and listen to your Hootie and the Blowfish records over and over until your ears bleed because of the hemorrhaging in your brain that happens when you've listened to "Let Her Cry" for the 999th time in a row!

I'm so over you.

Pretentious Record Store Guy's 50 Cool Band Names I Came Up With Today

What did you do today?

I listened to the entire Belle and Sebastian catalog on vinyl, and I came up with 50 cool band names. Then I had the whole afternoon to bask in my glory. Kind of beats your little 9 to 5 doesn't it?

So, here we go – **50 Cool Band Names I Came Up With Today**. You're welcome.

The Stares, No Exit, No Hope for Escape, Operator, There Is An Emergency, People Killing People, Kill Your Puppets, The Sesame Street Walkers, How Rudimentary My Dear Watson, Hare, Violens (not misspelled), Upstairs, Evil Jeans Us, Hasta La Quinta, Flight of the Deceiver, I Had a Burst of Brilliance the Other Day But You Rudely Interrupted Me Before I Could Write It Down Now I Will Be Forever Wondering What That Burst of Brilliance Was and If It Could Have Changed the Course of Mankind, Perhaps I Was Wrong, I Sincerely Doubt It, The Challengers, Are You Challenging Me, MIT Mouse (obviously mathcore), Stairing Contest (not misspelled), Blink F--k You Too (sounds kind of like 182), People Never Say Thank You Anymore, The Hell Handbasket, Ain't Nothing But A G String, The Sherlock Holmes Conspiracy, Twix, Resume, The Whoremones, Upstares, The Teenage Mutant Ninja Turtle Experience, The Power Transformers, Sir Cut Brakers, His Majestic Excellency Requests, El Magnifico, The Leather Strait Jackets, A Question of Taste, Stupid Pet Trick or Treat, Hello Queen, Thoughts of Suicide Pass Through My Mind But Your Memory Keeps Me Going, House of 1,000 Dead Petting Zoos, An Affair to Dismember, A Rivers Cuomo Runs Through It, Brad Pitfall, The Broken Dream Cast A Long Shadow, In the Light of Day You Aren't As Beautiful as You Used to Be, We Are Getting Older Now, Deaf Becomes Her...

And the number one band name is **Bleed the Blood of the Dying** -- even though I didn't come up with it today, it still deserves a place at the top of the pantheon of today's names because of its utter genius.

You have been warned.

Fuck Seth Cohen

If youre like me then you're 5'10", rail-thin, ridiculously good-looking, and your hair is the elixir from which dreams are made. You're also a pretentious music fan, an aficionado of the underground, the litmus test by which any band who is anyone will be judged and blogged by before their fist single even makes it to a mall to be sold at Sam Goody and purchased by know-nothings who will only buy whatever *Rolling Stone, Spin,* or *A.P.* advertisers steer them towards. We are the taste-makers that serve up our sacrificial lambs to the mainstream so that they can die and be resurrected in the temple of rock.

You might even watch *The O.C.*, which brings me to my point or rather to the question which I pose herein:

If an Indie band sold out on The O.C., *would there be any hipsters left to watch?*

More and more, every concert I go to is being populated by a litany of teens and preteens. I now find myself having to navigate the narrows of the pit with sinewy, gawky, 13-year-olds who are all elbows and acne, while their parents stand three feet behind me staring at me, silently judging me, while I drink my intoxicants and smoke my Camel lights. This has seriously begun to dampen my joy for the live show, a staple of my pretentious existence.

While I cannot hold this against the young, for we were all once preteen, unpretentious music lovers at one time or another before we became schooled in rock, I do hold one man personally responsible. That man is Seth Cohen.

Fuck Seth Cohen!

Seth Cohen has ruined my life! He has taken the one thing in the world that I hold dear and prostituted it for the world to take turns with and discard after their momentary desire is satisfied. He has taken a great many of my favorite Indie bands and served them up for the mainstream masses to suckle upon their teat. And, oh, how every band is lining up for their turn to bare their breasts!

Now I am all for spreading the word and getting great music heard, but at the same time, music is the one thing -- *the only thing*

- that I care about. Discovering a band is a very special thing. Getting in on the ground floor, being one of the first people at the concert who knows all the songs, meeting the band after the show and helping spread the word through the underground is an unequaled experience. When a band finally breaks into the mainstream, you feel some sort of satisfaction in knowing that you did your part to help them along the way; they will always be your own little special band.

Not anymore. Now every Thursday, Seth Cohen and *The O.C.* break my heart on the regular by serving up another one of my favorite bands to be gorged on and devoured by mainstream Teen America.

And each passing week I feel a little bit sadder, a little bit older, and my life a little bit more meaningless.

Thanks a lot, Seth Cohen.

If I could ever meet Seth Cohen, this is what I would say: "Go fuck yourself."

And I would punch him right in the face.

Yes, I know he's not real. But still, fuck that guy.

You Say You Want A Revolution...

"I think I might change up my style just to fit in." - Beastie Boys

What are you going to do? If you can't beat them, join them.

I'm talking about the MySpace and Me generation and all their emo-ness and cores.

I'm talking about **Bleed the Blood of the Dying**, the most awesomest, hipster post emo-core, post post-punk, slightly death metal band on the planet, and they're coming your way soon.

Enjoy the prelude, because the main feature will blow your mind ten ways from Tuesday.

Bleed the Blood of the Dying will soon take over the world. You heard it here first...

30 Most Underrated Albums of the Last 10 Years

What do critics know? Nothing, or else they would be in a band making music.

Fuck the critics, especially rock critics. Most of them are 30 to 40-year-olds, predominantly male, slightly balding sycophants, who live in their parents' basement and have little to no social interaction with the outside world and sit around listening to music all day because music is the only thing that fills the void in their meaningless existence.

Man, that hits a little too close to home, but I digress.

Anyway, here is my list of the **30 Most Underrated Albums of the Last Ten Years** (1996 - 2006). Enjoy.

1. Weezer - *Pinkerton*
2. Modest Mouse - *The Lonesome Crowded West*
3. Outkast - *ATLiens*
4. The Verve - *Urban Hymns*
5. Rage Against the Machine - *Evil Empire*
6. Evan Dando - *Baby I'm Bored*
7. Mos Def - *Black on Both Sides*
8. Ambulance LTD. - *Ambulance LTD.*
9. Muse - *Absolution*
10. The Dandy Warhols - *13 Tales from Urban Bohemia*
11. Vue - *Down for Whatever*
12. Q-Tip - *Kamal the Abstract*
13. The Stratford 4 - *Love & Distortion*
14. Clearlake - *Ceadars*
15. The Shins - *Oh Inverted World!*
16. Jesse Malin - *The Fine Art of Self Destruction*
17. The Dust Brothers - *Soundtrack to the motion picture Fight Club*
18. Mitch Hedberg - *Strategic Grill Locations*
19. Superdrag - *In the Valley of Dying Stars*
20. Goodie Mob - *Still Standing*
21. Ours - *Distorted Lullabies*
22. Palo Alto - *Heroes and Villains*
23. Pavement - *Brighten the Corners*
24. Josh Rouse - *1972*
25. Ugly Casanova - *Sharpen Your Teeth*
26. Ben Harper - *Live from Mars*
27. Rancid - *Life Won't Wait*
28. Harvey Danger - *King James Version*
29. Pinback - *Blue Screen Life*
30. Old 97s - *Too Far to Care*

Pretentious Record Store Guy's 50 ALL-NEW Cool Bands Names I Came Up with Today

What did you do today?

I listened to The Magnetic Fields' *69 Love Songs* in its entirety (Stephin Merritt should win a Nobel Peace Prize or something) on vinyl while drinking a Starbucks Caramel Frappacino, and then, because all my fans demanded it, I came up with *50 All-New Cool Band Names.* I would have had the whole afternoon to bask in my glory, but I had the closing shift at the record store so I had to deal with people like you all night long.

What? Not everyone is born rich; some of us have to work menial, laborious jobs until the world finally recognizes our utter genius.

Luckily, I don't have a menial, laborious job: I work at a record store. Kind of makes you wonder why you spent all your parents' money to go to college only to get a job that you despise. That's why when I thought of going to college, I dropped acid instead and thought about cool band names that I could eventually call my band whenever I got around to learning how to play the guitar my mom bought me for my 13th birthday. BTW, I just finished learning all the chords last year, so watch out, world!

Back to the point at hand, here we go – **Pretentious Record Store Guy's 50 All-New Cool Band Names I Came Up with Today.**

The Wholigans, Ty Died, If You Reap What You Sow Then Death Has Surely Got It Coming, Fine Whine (an emo band), White Swallow, Death from Dying, United Parcel Service, The Downs, Hermaphrodite Love Child, The Boxers Bat, Suicide by Cop, The On-Deck Circle Jerks, Dazed and Misused, Sue Me, The Imp Pencils, The Porno Graffiti, Lakeside Quartet, The Legal Department, Male Room, SmokeFireBurntSienna, Calamity Jane Doe, Ibuprofen, The Jesse James Gang Bang Band, Sexters, The Flasks, Alaska Is So Much Nicer In the Summer, August Cowboys, Serenity Now, The House Fire, A Forrest, Dee Mentioned, 13th Level Elfin Wizard, The Love Cats, Demon Slayer, Rest Assured, Dr. Scholl You Call Yourself a Doctor But You Couldn't Heel Me, You Are the One (Who Is the Liar?), Mercy Boo Coup, The George Washington Junior High School Fencing Team Tryouts, Sonic Boom Boom, Out of Touch (Out of Time), The Deals, The Fashionistas, Christopher Columbus Day Experiment, The Co-Pathetics, South by Southfist, Satan Has 8 Cocks and All of Them Are Evil, The Runners, Dying Machine, Tripping Acid in a Crowded Tent Isn't Really as Fun as It Sounds, Maybe I Should Have Gone to College...

And the number one band name is **The Snake Gang** – my all-new side project that is a down-and-dirty, country roots, rock band. I just came up with it this morning, and it still deserves a place at the top of the pantheon of today's names because it is so tough it makes Marlon Brando come back to life only to wet himself and run back to his eternal resting place whimpering about how he could have been someone.

You had your chance, Marlon. Now it's my turn.

Bleed the Blood of the Dying Bleeds No More...

I write this blog with a heavy heart: yesterday Bleed the Blood of the Dying broke up.

I can't realy talk about it now, because I was forced to sign a nondisclosure clause by Satan (by Satan I mean the mainstream record company whose name I cannot mention but is sort of like Washington, D.C.). But if I were to write about it, I would say that some people in the band (present company excluded) value money and mainstream suck-sess more than artistic integrity and indie credibility. Some people in the band (present company excluded) disagreed with the indie philosophy and spirit of which the band was initially formed. Some people in the band (present company excluded) thought that going on tour and opening up for Satan's (by Satan I mean once again the mainstream record company whose name I cannot mention) "Mall Punk Lite Summer Nites Tour" would be a great way to get our foot in the door and broaden our fan base. At least that is what Bob, Satan's minion, had told us, and some people in the band (present company excluded) fell for it hook, line, and sinker.

Finally, I would say that some people in the band (present company excluded) had to stuff their tight trousers with a tube sock before going onstage. Amatuers.

So what exactly happened?

Like I said before, I can't get into it now, but all I can say is that certain corporate sponsors thought that stopping Bleed the Blood of the Dying could be to their advantage, a position which I do not subscribe to. To these advertising whores I say, "Bleed the Blood of the Dying cannot be stopped; it cannot be contained; Bleed the Blood of the Dying is meant to flow free!"

But, alas, I am but one lone voice in a sea of red, which is paved in green, and seems so black.

So I did what I had to do.

I quit.

I quit because I will not compromise! I quit because I will not sell out! I quit because I want to be able to look my children in the eye one day and say, "The condom broke, and I still have my integrity!"

No worries, I've already moved on to bigger and better things. I'm in a new band now called **The Snake Gang**. We're an all-out rock and roll outfit, with a country flavor and dirty south blues influence. We only wear black, like Johnny Cash, and we only drink whiskey, like Hank Williams. Basically, we're going to reinvent American music by bringing music back to its gospel and blues roots, throwing in a little redneck charm with some urban, hipster ironic detachment while breaking out the acoustic guitars to 11.

We're like Christian Slater in *Heathers* but without the Jack Nicholson accent and with cowboy boots.

Except we're so much better-looking.

Snakes are the new skulls. 2005 was all about the Jolly Roger, but 2006 will be all about snakes. More specifically, The Snake Gang!

America: break out the snake bite kits and prepare to be poisoned by the venomous sounds of The Snake Gang!

You heard it here first, kids.

Your Alternative Station Is Such a Bankrupt Vibration

Sometimes silence is golden.

Sometimes you just want to be alone in your room with all your favorite vinyl records surrounding you on your floor.

Sometimes you just have to sit back and listen to the music, preferably shirtless and in your underwear or your favoirte tight pants.

Tonight is definitely one of those nights.

Is there a better record than *Revolver*?

Lennon was right, happiness is a warm gun... spinning on your record player.

This Is Not an Ad for Pretentious Record Store Guy T-Shirts

If you were cool, you'd already have one. I have three, and I don't even wear them.

But you are not cool.

You probably like Phil Collins.

You probably think that drummers who step out from behind the drum kit aren't all egomaniacs who can't stand being kept in the back.

You probably would note the fact that said drummer always puts his fat, ugly mug on the cover of his record as an attempt to catalog his life at a specific point in time, a snapshot revealed in full through song and album art.

You probably sing along to "St-st-studio" but say it like "Su-Su-Studio" when you were in the shower.

You probably also like Don Henley's solo stuff.

That's why you're not cool.

Go back to elemenatary school when your life had meaning and you believed everything your parents ever told you, like the fact that Phil Collins was cool.

Parents are cruel.

Mother, May I Trust Pretentious Record Store Guy?

Q. What do Paul Simon, ladies' jeans, hipster battles, trust-fund hippies, The Action and fair-weather fans all have in common?

A. They all made a cameo appearance in *Pretentious Record Store Guy*.

Who's better? Who's best? Pete Best? Why, he's the original drummer for The Beatles and could only be replaced by a Starr.

Speaking of originality, there is a comic that is a complete ripoff of Abbott and Costello's classic routine "Who's on First," which was voted the best comedy routine of the 20th according to *Time* magazine. But Abbott and Costello simply caught the gag that had been floating through the smoke-filled air of certain vaudeville theatres for quite some time, which proves that all good art is theft.

Come to think of it, isn't good theft an art?

Here's to the ghosts of the 20th century who continue to haunt us to this very day.

Guess who?

Take the pill, buy the ticket, and enjoy the drive by...

Long live Elvis Presley, Chuck Berry, Little Richard, and John Lennon!

Praise be to Brian Jones!

Praise be to Andrew Wood!

Long live Rock and Roll!

An Archipelago of Pet Sounds

So what's up, people? How has life been treating you? I know I've been underground for a while now (my bad), but I have been busy working hard to entertain you.

I've been locked away like a hermit, at a cabin in Minnesota which serves as our studio, with the rest of The Snake Gang, recording our self-titled debut album with Steve Albini's engineer's former intern, Gary Nash. He was with Steve's engineer during the Big Black, Pixies, and Nirvana sessions, but left before Steve produced Bush's second record (thank God for that).

Anyway, Gary has invented this whole new wa to record that is sort of like Phil Spector's "Wall of Sound," except different. He's calling it the "Archipelago of Sound" because, and I quote, "it's like you're a body of land that is surrounded on three sides by water, except in this case it's sound." When I told him that he just described what is a "peninsula," he got mad, threw a microphone at my head, and to me that without him I would just be a writer o music that tampon companies would use in their commercials. I couldn't argue with his logic, so I am now down with the "Archipelag of Sound." Besides, archipelago sounds way better than peninsula.

The resulting album is like *Songs About Fucking* meets *Surfer Rosa*, but definitely nothing like *Razorblade Suitcase*. All of you file-sharing motherfuckers are going to have wait until we go on tour for The Snake Gang t strangle you with our sound and wrap our music around your earholes. We're going to b the new Velvet Underground, except without Nico, not from New York, a little more alt-country, and completely different!

Whatever. The point is that when the other guys in the band were recording their parts (and then rerecording their parts and then re-rerecording their parts because they really don't know how to play their instruments, and the only reason I even hired them for the ban was because they looked cool and would ben to my will), I made a graphic novel of what le me up to that point in time.

This is the soundtrack to the autobiography o the story of my life (printed on dead trees).

You should read it. If you've already read it, you should read it again to see if you missed anything the first time.

You always miss the first time.

Enjoy.

EDITOR'S NOTE: These writings appeared in various forms and forums from 2005 to 2008

The Action
Rolled Gold

Ryan Adams
Heartbreaker

Ryan Adams
Gold

Alice in Chains
Dirt

Alice in Chains
Jar of Flies

Ambulance LTD
Ambulance LTD

The Anniversary
Designing a Nervous Breakdown

The Anniversary
Your Majesty

Arcade Fire
Funeral

Arcade Fire
Neon Bible

Arcade Fire
The Suburbs

Nic Armstrong
The Greatest White Liar

Art Brut
Bang, Bang, Rock and Roll

Art Brut
Art Brut vs. Satan

Richard Ashcroft
Alone with Everyone

At the Drive-In
Relationship of Command

Avalanches
Since I Left You

Badfinger
The Very Best of

Eyrkah Badu
Baduizm

Eyrkah Badu
Mama's Gun

The Band
Music From Big Pink

The Band
The Band

Beastie Boys
Licensed to Ill

Beastie Boys
Paul's Boutique

Beastie Boys
Check Your Head

Beastie Boys
Ill Communication

The Beatles
A Hard Day's Night

The Beatles
Rubber Soul

The Beatles
Revolver

The Beatles
Sgt. Pepper's Lonely Hearts Club Band

The Beatles
The Beatles

The Beatles
Abbey Road

The Beatles
Let It Be

Beck
Odelay

Beck
Midnite Vultures

Belle & Sebastian
If You're Feeling Sinister

Belle & Sebastian
The Boy with the Arab Strap

Belle & Sebastian
Dear Catastrophe Waitress

The Bens
The Bens

Chuck Berry
The Great Twenty-Eight

Big Star
#1 Record

Big Star
Radio City

Black Rebel Motorcyle Club
B.R.M.C.

Black Rebel Motorcycle Club
Howl

Black Rebel Motorcycle Club
Baby 81

Black Rebel Motorcyle Club
Beat the Devil's Tattoo

Blind Melon
Soup

Blind Melon
Nico

Bloc Party
Silent Alarm

Bloc Party
Weekend in the City

Bloc Party
Intimacy

Blondie
Parallel Lines

Blondie
The Best of Blondie

Blur
Parklife

Blur
Blur

Blur
13

David Bowie
Ziggy Stardust

David Bowie
Alladin Sane

David Bowie
Diamond Dogs

David Bowie
Low

David Bowie
Heroes

Brian Jonestown Massacre
Strung Out in Heaven

Brian Jonestown Massacre
Tepid Peppermint Wonderland

Bright Eyes
Lifted or the Story Is...

Bright Eyes
I'm Wide Awake, It's Morning

James Brown
Live at the Appllo

James Brown
Sex Machine

James Brown
20 All-Time Greatest Hits

Built to Spill
Perfect from Now On

Built to Spill
Keep It Like a Secret

Built to Spill
Live

The Byrds
Sweethearts of the Rodeo

Calla
Collisions

Camp-Lo
Uptown Saturday Night

The Cardigans
Gran Tourismo

The Cardigans
Super Heavy Extra Gravity

The Cars
Complete Greatest Hits

The Chameleons
Return of the Roughnecks

Cheap Trick
Essential Cheap Trick

The Church
Under the Milky Way

The Clash
The Clash

The Clash
London Calling

The Clash
Sandanista

The Clash
Live on Broadway

Jimmy Cliff
The Harder They Come

Clipse
Lord Willin'

Clipse
Hell Hath No Fury

John Coltrane
Blue Train

John Coltrane
Giant Steps

John Coltrane
A Love Supreme

Common Sense
Resurrection

Common
One Day It'll All Make Sense

Common
Electric Circus

Common
Be

Sam Cooke
Greatest Hits

Cornelius
Fantasma

Cornelius
Point

Elvis Costello
My Aim Is True

Elvis Costello
This Year's Model

Elvis Costello
Get Happy!!

Counting Crows
August and Everything After

Counting Crows
Recovering the Satellites

CSS
Cansei de Ser Sexy

The Cure
Pornography

The Cure
Disintegration

Cursive
Domestica

D'Angelo
Brown Sugar

D'Angelo
Voodoo

Daft Punk
Homework

Daft Punk
Discovery

Evan Dando
Live from the Brattle

Evan Dando
Baby I'm Bored

The Dandy Warhols
The Dandy's Rule OK

The Dandy Warhols
Come Down

The Dandy Warhols
13 Tales from Urban Bohemi

The Dandy Warhols
Welcome to the Monkey Hou

Miles Davis
Birth of the Cool

Miles Davis
Round About Midnight

Miles Davis
Kind of Blue

Miles Davis
Bitches Brew

Dead Prez
Let's Get Free

Death from Above 1979
You're a Woman...

De La Soul
3ft High and Rising

De La Soul
De La Soul Is Dead

Del the Funky Homosapien
I Wish My Brother George...

Del the Funky Homosapien
No Cause for Alarm

Del the Funky Homosapien
Both Sides of the Brain

Deltron 3030
Deltron 3030

Desaparecidos
Read Music/Speak Spanish

Devo
Q: Are We Not Men?

Devo
Freedom of Choice

Digable Planets
Reachin'

Dinosaur Jr.
Where You Been

Dinosaur Jr.
Without a Sound

DJ Shadow
Endtroducing

Django Django
Django Django

The Doors
The Doors

The Doors
L.A. Woman

The Doves
Lost Souls

Dr. Dre
The Chronic

Dr. Dre
2001

Nick Drake
Pink Moon

Dust Brothers
Fight Club (Soundtrack)

Bob Dylan
The Freewheeling' Bob Dylan

Bob Dylan
The Times They Are A-Changin'

Bob Dylan
Highway 61 Revisited

Bob Dylan
Blonde on Blonde

Bob Dylan
Blood on the Tracks

Bob Dylan
Live 1966, Royal Albert Hall

Bob Dylan
Live 1975, Rolling Thunder

Bob Dylan & The Band
The Basement Tapes

The Eagles
The Very Best of

Easy-E
Eazy-Duz-It

Editors
The Back Room

Editors
An End Has a Start

Elastica
Elastica

Elefant
Sunlight Makes Me Paranoid

Elefant
Black Magic Show

Brian Eno
Here Come the Warm Jets

Brian Eno
Another Green World

EPMD
Strictly Business

Eric B. & Rakim
Classic

50 Cent
Get Rich or Die Trying

The Faint
Dance Macabre

Lupe Fiasco
Food & Liquor

Flying Burrito Bros.
Gilded Palace/Burrito Deluxe

Ben Folds Five
Whatever and Ever Amen

Ben Folds Five
...Reinhold Messner

Fountains of Wayne
Fountains of Wayne

Fountains of Wayne
Utopia Parkway

Franz Ferdinand
Franz Ferdinand

French Kicks
One Time Bells

Fugazi
Repeater + 3 Songs

Fugees
The Score

G. Love and Special Sauce
Yeah, It's That Easy

Gang of Four
That's Entertainment

Gang Starr
Step in the Arena

Gang Starr
Moment of Truth

Marvin Gaye
What's Going On

Marvin Gaye
Let's Get It On

Gnarls Barkley
St. Elsewhere

Golden Smog
Weird Tales

The Good The Bad & The Queen
The Good The Bad & The Queen

Goodie Mobb
Still Standing

Gorrillaz
Gorrillaz

Gorrillaz
Demon Days

Al Green
Greatest Hits Vol. I

Guns N' Roses
Appetite for Destruction

Guns N' Roses
Lies

Guns N' Roses
Use Your Illusion I & II

GZA
Liquid Swords

Anthony Hamilton
Coming from Where I'm From

Herbie Hancock
Essential Herbie Hancock

Herbie Hancock
Blue Note Sixties Sessions

Ben Harper
Fight for Your Mind

Ben Harper
Live from Mars

George Harrison
All Things Must Pass

Harvey Danger
Where Have All the Merrymakers Gone?

Harvey Danger
King James Version

Harvey Danger
Little by Little

Jimi Hendrix
Are You Experienced

Jimi Hendrix
Axis: Bold as Love

Jimi Hendrix
Electric Ladyland

Hieroglyphics
3rd Eye Vision

Hieroglyphics
Full Circle

Lauryn Hill
The Miseducation of...

The Hives
Veni Vidi Vicious

The Hold Steady
Boys and Girls in America

Hole
Live Through This

Billie Holiday
Essential Billie Holiday

Ice Cube
AmeriKKKa's Most Wanted

Ice Cube
The Predator

Iggy and the Stooges
Raw Power

Iggy Pop
The Idiot

Iggy Pop
Lust for Life

International Noise Conspiracy
Survival Sickness

Interpol
Turn on the Bright Lights

Interpol
Antics

Michael Jackson
Off the Wall

Michael Jackson
Thriller

The Jackson 5
The Ultimate Collection

The Jam
In the City

The Jam
This Is the Modern World

The Jam
All Mods Con

Etta James
At Last!

Jane's Addiction
Nothing's Shocking

Jane's Addiction
Ritual de lo Habitual

The Jayhawks
Tomorrow the Green Grass

The Jayhawks
Rainy Day Music

Jay-Z
Reasonable Doubt

Jonathan Fire*Eater
Wolf Songs for Lambs

Robert Johnson
The Complete Recordings

Jurassic Five
Quality Control

Jurassic Five
Power in Numbers

King of Convenience
Quiet Is the New Loud

Kings of Leon
Youth and Young Manhood

The Kinks
The Kinks

The Kinks
Village Green

The Kinks
Arthur

The Kinks
Lola Versus Powerman

Talib Kweli
Quality

Talib Kweli & Hi-Tek
Train of Thought

Ben Kweller
Sha Sha

Ben Kweller
On My Way

Ben Kweller
Ben Kweller

Kyuss
Muchas Gracias

Led Zeppelin
I

Led Zeppelin
II

Led Zeppelin
IV

The Lemonheads
Lovey

The Lemonheads
It's a Shame About Ray

The Lemonheads
Come on Feel...

John Lennon
Plastic Ono Band

John Lennon
Imagine

Mad Season
Above

Madlib
Blunted in the Bomb Shelter

Madlib
Shades of Blue

Madvillain
Madvillainy

The Magnetic Fields
69 Love Songs

The Magnetic Fields
i

Jesse Malin
The Fine Art of Self Destructi

Jesse Malin
The Heat

Bob Marley
Songs of Freedom

Marilyn Manson
Antichrist Superstar

Material Issue
International Pop Overthrow

Maxwell
Urban Hang Suite

Paul McCartney
Wingspan: Hits & History

Method Man
Tical

Method Man/Redman
Blackout!

Minor Threat
The Complete Discography

The Misfits
Colection

The Modern Lovers
The Modern Lovers

Modest Mouse
The Lonesome Crowdest Wes

Modest Mouse
The Moon and Antartica

Modest Mouse
We Were Dead Before the Ship Even Sank

Thelonius Monk
Blue Note Sessions

Van Morrison
Astral Weeks

Van Morrison
Moondance

Mos Def
Black on Both Sides

Mos Def & Talib Kweli
Are Black Star

Mother Love Bone
Mother Love Bone

Murder City Devils
Empty Bottles Broken Hearts

Muse
Origin of Symmetry

Muse
Absolution

Muse
Black Holes and Revelations

My Bloody Valentine
Loveless

My Morning Jacket
It Still Moves

My Morning Jacket
Z

Nada Surf
High/Low

Nada Surf
The Proximity Effect

Nada Surf
Let Go

Nas
Illmatic

Nas
It Was Written

The National
Alligator

Neutral Milk Hotel
In an Aeroplane Over the Sea

New Order
(The Best of)

The New Pornographers
Electric Version

The New Pornographers
Twin Cinema

A.C. Newman
The Slow Wonder

Nico
Chelsea Girl

Nine Inch Nails
Pretty Hate Machine

Nine Inch Nails
The Downward Spiral

Nirvana
Nevermind

Nirvana
In Utero

Nirvana
MTV Unplugged in New York

Notorious BIG
Ready to Die

Notorious BIG
Life After Death

Nouvelle Vague
Nouvelle Vague

NWA
Straight Outta Compton

Oasis
Definitely Maybe

Oasis
Morning Glory

Old 97s
Too Far Too Care

Operation Ivy
Operation Ivy

Outkast
ATLiens

Outkast
Aquemeni

Outkast
Stankonia

Outkast
Speakerboxxx/Love Below

Jimmy Page
Live at the Greek

Paloalto
Paloalto

Paloalto
Heroes & Villains

Parliament
Funked Up: The Very Best of

Gram Parsons
The Gram Parsons Anthology

Pavement
Slanted and Enchanted

Pavement
Crooked Rain, Crooked Rain

Pavement
Brighten the Corners

Pearl Jam
Ten

Pearl Jam
Vs.

Pearl Jam
Vitalogy

Pearl Jam
Live on Two Legs

Tom Petty
Wildflowers

Tom Petty & the Heartbreakers
Greatest Hits

Pigeonhead
The Full Sentence

Pinback
Blue Screen Life

Pink Floyd
Dark Side of the Moon

Pink Floyd
Wish You Were Here

Pink Floyd
The Wall

Pixies
Surfer Rosa

Pixies
Doolittle

Pixies
Bossanova

Pixies
Trompe le Monde

The Police
Outlandos D'Amour

Postal Service
Give Up

Elvis Presley
Elvis Presley

Elvis Presley
Essential Elvis Presley

Prince
Prince

Prince
Dirty Mind

Prince
1999

Prince and the Revolution
Purple Rain

Prince Paul
A Prince Among Thieves

Pulp
This Is Hardcore

Q-Tip
Amplified

Q-Tip
The Renaissance

Queens of the Stone Age
Rated R

Queens of the Stone Age
Songs for the Deaf

Radio 4
Gotham!

Radiohead
The Bends

Radiohead
OK Computer

Radiohead
Hail to the Thief

Radiohead
In Rainbows

Rage Against the Machine
Rage Against the Machine

Rage Against the Machine
Evil Empire

Rage Against the Machine
Renegades

The Rain Band
The Rain Band

The Rakes
Capture/Release

Rancid
Let's Go

Rancid
...And Out Come the Wolves

Rancid
Life Won't Wait

Red Hot Chili Peppers
What Hits!?

Red Hot Chili Peppers
Blood Sugar Sex Magik

Red Hot Chili Peppers
Californication

Otis Redding
The Very Best of

Lou Reed
Transformer

Refused
The Shape of Punk to Come

Remy Zero
Villa Elaine

The Rentals
Return of the Rentals

The Rentals
7 More Minutes

The Replacements
Let It Be

The Replacements
Tim

The Replacements
Pleased to Meet Me

The Replacements
Don't Tell a Soul

Rilo Kiley
More Adventurous

Pete Rock and C.L. Smooth
Mecca and the Soul Brother

Rogue Wave
Asleep at Heaven's Gate

Rolling Stones
Aftermath

Rolling Stones
Beggar's Banquet

Rolling Stones
Let It Bleed

Rolling Stones
Sticky Fingers

Rolling Stones
Exile on Main St.

The Roots
Things Fall Apart

The Roots
Phrenology

Josh Rouse
1972

Roxy Music
Country Life

Roxy Music
Siren

RZA
Bobby Digital in Stereo

Sex Pistols
Never Mind the Bollocks...

Remy Shand
The Way I Feel

The Shins
Oh Inverted World

The Shins
Chutes Too Narrow

Frank Sinatra
Greatest Hits Vol. I & II

Smashing Pumpkins
Gish

Smashing Pumpkins
Siamese Dream

Elliott Smith
Either/Or

Elliott Smith
XO

The Smiths
The Smiths

The Smiths
The Queen Is Dead

The Smiths
Strangeways Here We Come

Snoop Doggy Dogg
Doggystyle

Social Distortion
Social Distortion

Social Distortion
Somewhere Between Heaven and Hell

Son Volt
Trace

Son Volt
Straightaways

Son Volt
Wide Swing Tremolo

Sonic Youth
Daydream Nation

Sonic Youth
Dirty

Souls of Mischief
93' to Infinity

The Soundtrack of Our Lives
Extended Revelation...

The Soundtrack of Our Lives
Behind the Music

Spoon
Girls Can Tell

Spoon
Kill the Moonlight

Bruce Springsteen
Born to Run

Bruce Springsteen
Born in the USA

The Stills
Logic Will Break Your Heart

The Stills
Oceans Will Rise

The Stooges
The Stooges

The Stooges
Fun House

Stone Temple Pilots
Core

Stone Temple Pilots
Purple

Stratford 4
Revolt Against Tired Noise

Stratford 4
Love and Distortion

The Strokes
Is This It?

The Strokes
Room on Fire

The Strokes
First Impressions of Earth

Suede
Dog Man Star

Suede
Coming Up

Superdrag
Regrettfully Yours

Superdrag
A Headtrip in Every Key

Superdrag
In the Valley of Dying Stars

Swervedriver
Juggernaut Rides '89-'98

2Pac
Strictly for My N.I.G.G.A.Z.

2Pac
Me Against the World

2Pac
All Eyez on Me

Talking Heads
77

Talking Heads
More Songs About Buildings and Food

Talking Heads
Fear of Music

Talking Heads
Remain in Light

Television
Marquee Moon

Temple of the Dog
Temple of the Dog

The Thermals
Fuckin' A

The Thrills
So Much for the City

The Thrills
Let's Bottle Bohemia

The Toadies
Hell Below/Stars Above

Tool
Opiate

Tool
Undertow

Tool
Ænima

Traveling Wilburys
Vol. 1

A Tribe Called Quest
Low End Theory

A Tribe Called Quest
Midnight Marauders

A Tribe Called Quest
Beats, Rhymes & Life

U2
The Joshua Tree

Ugly Casanova
Sharpen Your Teeth

Uncle Tupelo
No Depression

Uncle Tupelo
Still Feel Gone

Uncle Tupelo
March 16-20, 1992

Uncle Tupelo
Anodyne

UNKLE
Psyence Fiction

Van Halen
Van Halen

Van Halen
II

Van Halen
MCMLXXXIV

Velvet Underground
White Heat/White Light

Velvet Underground
Loaded

Velvet Underground & Nico
Velvet Underground & Nico

Verve
A Storm in Heaven

Verve
Northern Soul

Verve
Urban Hymns

Violent Femmes
Add It Up (1981-1993)

Vue
Find Your Home

Vue
Down for Whatever

The Walkmen
Everyone Who Pretended to Like Me Is Gone

The Walkmen
You & Me

Weezer
Weezer

Weezer
Pinkerton

Paul Westerberg
14 Songs

Paul Westerberg
Stereo & Mono

Whiskeytown
Strangers Almanac

Whiskeytown
Pneumonia

The White Stripes
De Stijl

The White Stripes
White Blood Cells

The Who
My Generation

The Who
Who's Next

Wilco
Being There

Wilco
Summerteeth

Wilco
Yankee Hotel Foxtrot

Amy Winehouse
Back to Black

Wire
Pink Flag

Wu-Tang Clan
Enter the Wu-Tang Clan

The XX
The XX

Young Bleed
My Balls and My Word

Neil Young
Harvest Moon

Neil Young
Rust Never Sleeps

Thom Yorke
The Eraser

THE PLAYBACK YEARS

Pretentious Record Store Guy made its debut in *Playback:STL* in March 2005. The first six or seven strips were don in a much more simplified and cartoony style that I liked at the time, but looking back on it now seems like a poor decision. I don't think I was as confident in allowing my art to tell the story as I am today. Granted, I still think my art is generally the worst part of my stories, but that's my cross to bear. Unfortunately, my computer crashed that summer so I actually lost the first six strips I ever did. Fortunately, I had saved all of the scripts to a floppy disk...

PRETENTIOUS RECORD STORE GUY

Happy Holidays! **BY CARLOS RUIZ**

...The moral of the story? Story prevails.

In the beginning, I was much more concerned with building up the first few panels in order to make the joke land. As the strip progressed, I started letting the story flow in ways I had not previously. Each strip became a way to show all the crazy, funny, music-obsessed, and conspiracy theory-laden discussions that record store clerks had. My buddy Ryan Shaw told me about his "Andrew Wood as the Grunge Messiah" theory, and I knew I had to use it (so I asked him for permission). Suddenly, the strips began to look more realistic and the panel design started to shift from strip to strip.

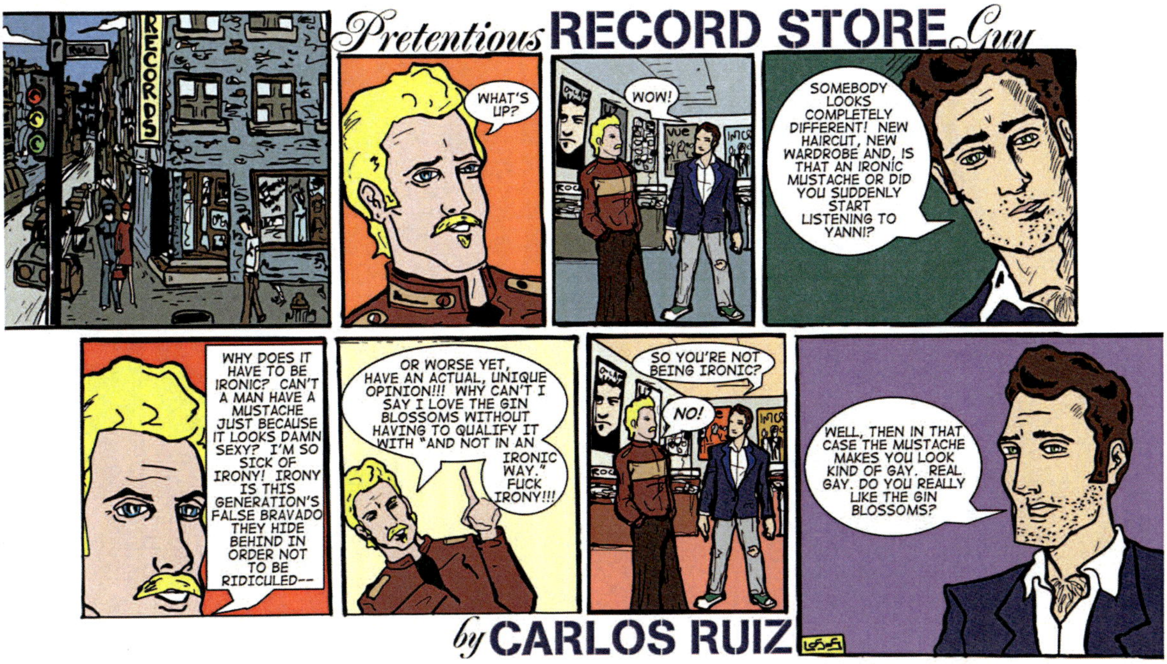

THE PLAYBACK YEARS

Every March, *Playback* would head down to SXSW in Austin for their annual (epic) issue based around the festival. In anticipation of the issue, I decided that Guy and his new fake band, Bleed the Blood of the Dying, would also be making their own pilgrimage down to Texas as their indie right of passage. Bands on the road, trapped in a van, playing small clubs to indifferent audiences of five or six people, what could go wrong? At that point, the story ended up writing itself.

What if the joke became real, and no one realized you were joking to begin with? Worse yet, what if it ended up being a success? At what point do you bail? Or *do* you bail? Do you ride the wave? If you don't care, does it matter?

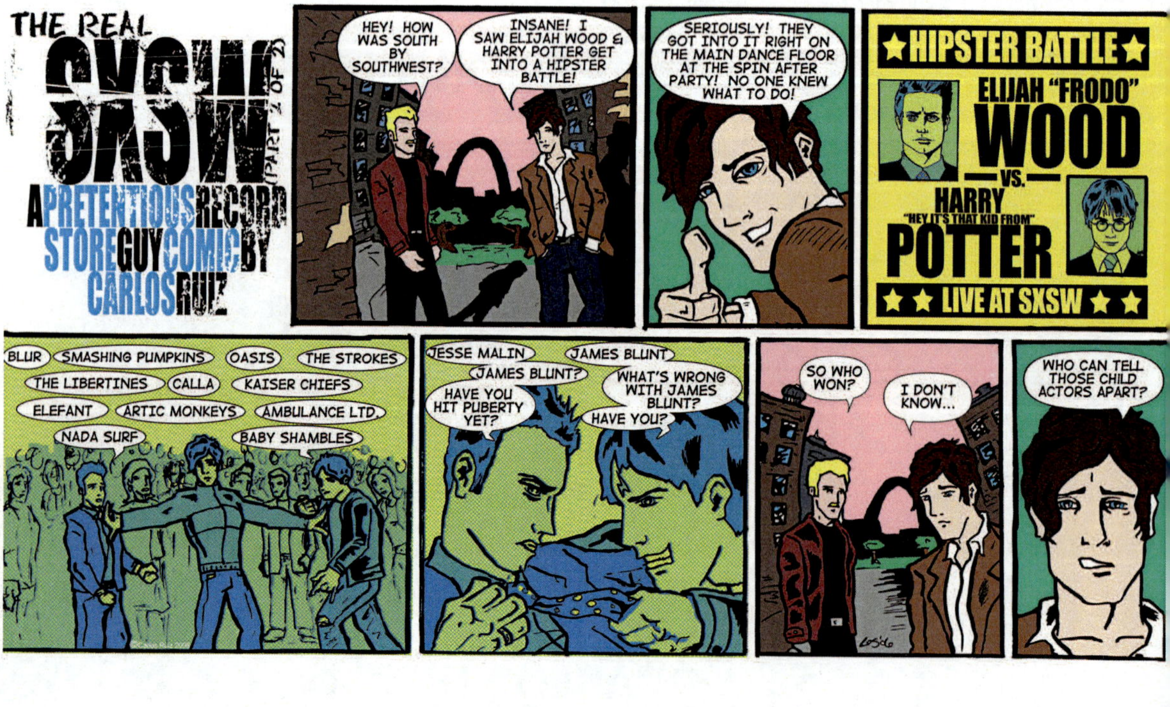

I liked having Guy get everything he thought he wanted, only not the way he thought it would happen. Isn't that just a kick in the teeth? "The Record Deal" still remains my all-time favorite *Pretentious Record Store Guy* strip. Why? Maybe it's the beat that he waits, taking it all in, knowing what his decision is ultimately going to be, before he answers the suit. Classic Guy. Everything matters.

So it was around this point that I knew the end was near. I liked doing the strip. I was actually happy with the way the art was turning out, and the story had an ending I dug. I knew right then that I had to make a miniseries to expand on the story because the strips were no longer enough to contain the pretentiousness. The journey was done.

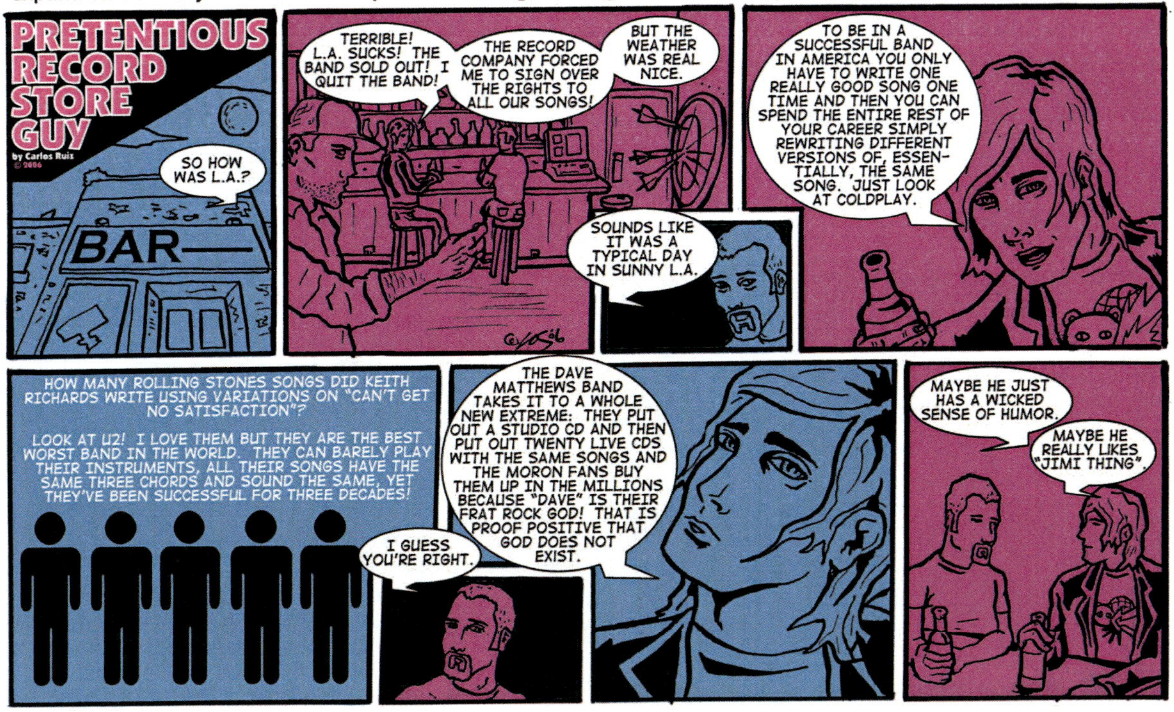

THE PLAYBACK YEARS

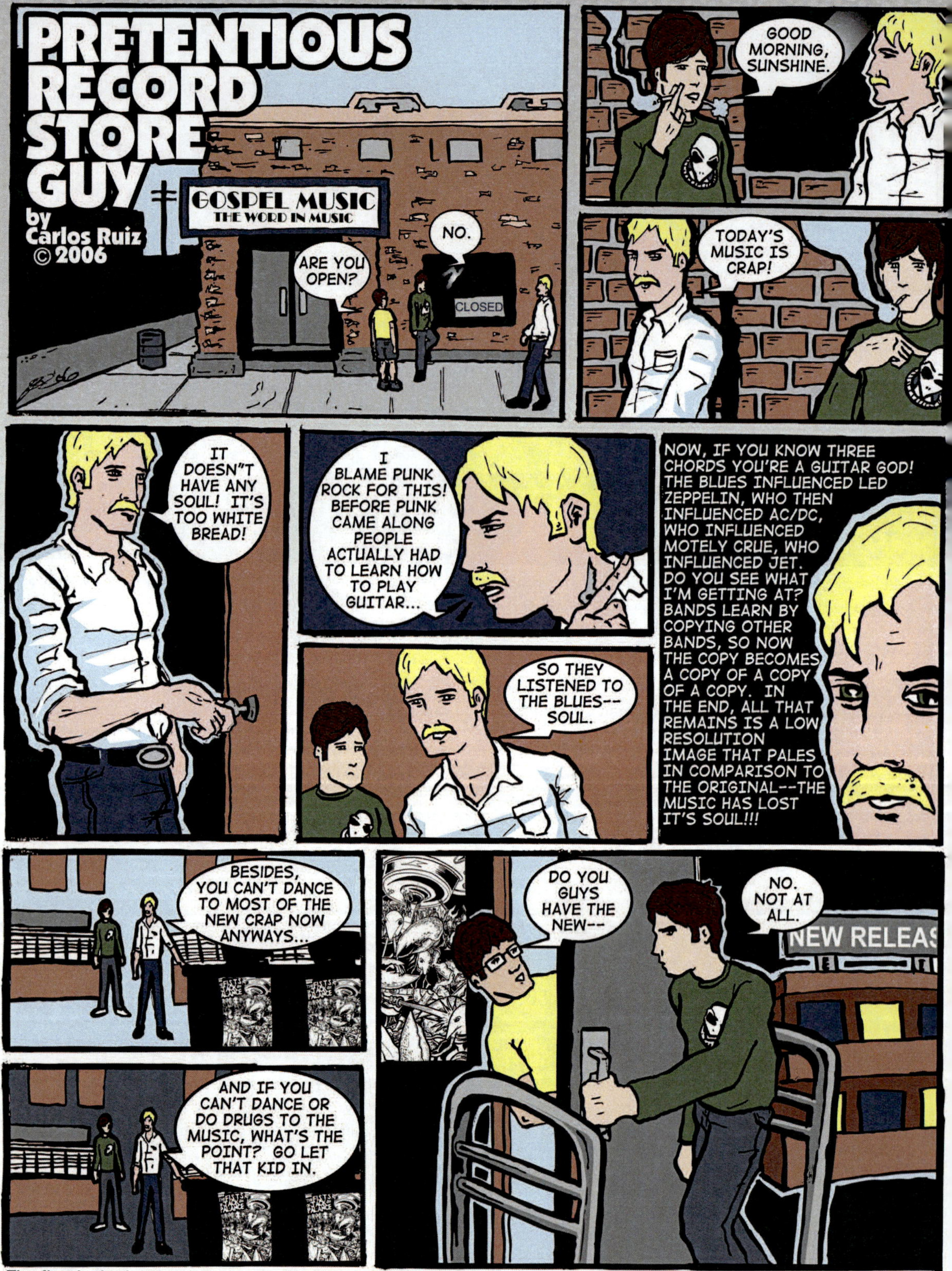

The first is the last, and the last is the first. This was the last *Pretentious Record Store Guy* strip that ran in *Playback:STL* and is actually where the first issue of the miniseries kicks off. How fitting that it is now the last strip in the *Pretentious Record Store Guy* collection. A perfect little piece of symmetry pie. The end is the start is THE END.

SPECIAL THANKS

This book couldn't have been possible without the support of the following people.

First and foremost, I want to say thanks to my family for their unconditional love and support. To my mom and dad for letting me spend way to much time drawing and reading comics when I was younger and not batting an eye when I told them I wanted to major in art. To my wife and son for letting me escape to my own fortress of solitude, my upstairs office, to make comics.

Thanks to Dr. DJ Frye for telling me I should be an aritst. To Frank Stack for showing me how to really make comics. To all the art teachers and professors I've had who've helped inspire me to become an artist (in order): Mrs. Bonelli, Mr. Johnson, Mrs. Mitchell, Dr. Frye, Brooke Cameron, Frank Stack, Bill Hawk and Mark Langeneckert.

Thanks to Dan Tylkowski and Julie Seabaugh for giving me my first comic strip gig in a "real" magazine, *Two Drink Minimum.*

Thanks to Jim Dunn and Laura Hamlett for first taking a chance on *Pretentious Record Store Guy* and publishing it in pages of *Playback: STL.*

Thanks to Brian Azzarello for all the great conversation, advice, and inspiration.

Thanks to Bryan A. Hollerbach for helping me compile and editing all my nonsense into a semi-legible form. To Jason Green, my former editor at *Playback:STL* and now my fellow editor at Ink and Drink Comics, for always providing a fresh set of eyes and different perspective. To Steve Higgins for always surprising me and never getting too mad at me.

Thanks to all of the Ink and Drink Comics crew for helping start a scene that needed to be seen. I'm proud of how far we've come and all of the great work you do.

Thanks to all the people who helped make this book possible with the Kickstarter campaign. A special thank-you goes to all of the Cornerstone Kickstarter members and above for their support. Thanks to Adrian Arroyo, Brian Atkins, Sam Belfeuil, Rich "RichVGS" Bergin, David Blue, Chrissy, Brady and Ana Clark, Jennifer Clement and Ben Mohler, Paul Colombo, Adam Daughhetee, Brent and Beth Ecenbarger, Luke Elrod, Renee Rold Godbee, Grain Audio, Jason Green, Andy Halleen, Walker Hamilton, Steve Higgins, Erin Jameson, Justin Jarrett, Jerry, Kahaleed, David David Katzman, Mike Kennedy, Brooks Kickham, Sarah Janelle Kunza, Eileen Long, JR Narayan, Lisa Robin Nelson, Jameson O'Guinn, Michael Parr, Julian "JR" Robinson, Kevin Rubin, Amy Ruiz, Carlos E. and Ana A. Ruiz, Gardito Ruiz, Tom Schairer, Julie Seabaugh, Justin Lee Siemer, Eden Stanton, Corey Tadlock, Thomas Lewis, Dan Tylkowski, Todd Williamson, www.absolutionprints.com, and Bryan "Cupcakes" Wygal.

Finally, thanks to Palmer Shiers for giving me a mixtape with The Smiths, James, The Cure, and The Lemonheads on it. It was game over after that.

carlos gabriel ruiz is a writer, illustrator, designer, and art director based in St. Louis. He is the creator of *Pretentious Record Store Guy* and *Parade of Freaks*. He was a finalist on DC Comics' Zuda website with the submission *Development Hell* in 2007. *Shorts + Losses* and *The Baron Age*, with collaborator Jim Mosley, are his latest works. Currently he is working on the autobiographical comic *Comic-Con-A-Sewer* and the graphic novel *The Revengers*. Carlos graduated from the University of Missouri with a BFA in painting and drawing. His work can be found online at **carlosgabrielruiz.com** and at **paradeoffreaks.com**.

www.braincloudcomics.com